ALLEN COUNTY PUBLIC LIBRARY

REA

3 1833 0

P9-DTL-189

"I Don't Know Why You Hide Yourself, Lane, But I See It," Tyler Said.

Lane wasn't going to ask what he saw. It would erect barriers she didn't want right now. That should have warned her, but she ignored the warnings.

"And instead of my dreams haunting me with what making love to you might be like, I have that to keep me company."

She blinked. "You dream of me. Of us?"

"Oh, yeah."

Lane didn't think she could be more stunned. And more pleased. She'd given him absolutely no reason to think she wanted more, and here he was, making her feel incredibly sexy and wanted.

"I want to strip you down right now and taste every inch of you, but I won't. We won't. Not tonight."

"That implies there will be another night."

He smiled. "I was hoping you'd caught that…."

ROMANCE

DEC 1 5 2003

Dear Reader,

Thank you for choosing Silhouette Desire—where passion is guaranteed in every read. Things sure are heating up with our continuing series DYNASTIES: THE BARONES. Eileen Wilks's *With Private Eyes* is a powerful romance that helps set the stage for the daring conclusion next month. And if it's more continuing stories that you want— we have them. TEXAS CATTLEMAN'S CLUB: THE STOLEN BABY launches this month with Sara Orwig's *Entangled with a Texan*.

The wonderful Peggy Moreland is on hand to dish up her share of Texas humor and heat with *Baby, You're Mine*, the next installment of her TANNERS OF TEXAS series. Be sure to catch Peggy's Silhouette Single Title, *Tanner's Millions*, on sale January 2004. Award-winning author Jennifer Greene marks her much-anticipated return to Silhouette Desire with *Wild in the Field*, the first book in her series THE SCENT OF LAVENDER.

Also for your enjoyment this month, we offer Katherine Garbera's second book in the KING OF HEARTS series. *Cinderella's Christmas Affair* is a fabulous "it could happen to you" plot guaranteed to leave her fans extremely satisfied. And rounding out our selection of delectable stories is *Awakening Beauty* by Amy J. Fetzer, a steamy, sensational tale.

More passion to you!

Melissa Jeglinski

Melissa Jeglinski
Senior Editor, Silhouette Desire

Please address questions and book requests to:
Silhouette Reader Service
U.S.: 3010 Walden Ave., P.O. Box 1325, Buffalo, NY 14269
Canadian: P.O. Box 609, Fort Erie, Ont. L2A 5X3

Awakening Beauty

AMY J. FETZER

Published by Silhouette Books
America's Publisher of Contemporary Romance

If you purchased this book without a cover you should be aware
that this book is stolen property. It was reported as "unsold and
destroyed" to the publisher, and neither the author nor the
publisher has received any payment for this "stripped book."

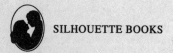 **SILHOUETTE BOOKS**

ISBN 0-373-76548-7

AWAKENING BEAUTY

Copyright © 2003 by Amy J. Fetzer

All rights reserved. Except for use in any review, the reproduction
or utilization of this work in whole or in part in any form by any
electronic, mechanical or other means, now known or hereafter
invented, including xerography, photocopying and recording, or in
any information storage or retrieval system, is forbidden without
the written permission of the editorial office, Silhouette Books,
233 Broadway, New York, NY 10279 U.S.A.

All characters in this book have no existence outside the imagination of
the author and have no relation whatsoever to anyone bearing the same
name or names. They are not even distantly inspired by any individual
known or unknown to the author, and all incidents are pure invention.

This edition published by arrangement with Harlequin Books S.A.

® and TM are trademarks of Harlequin Books S.A., used under license.
Trademarks indicated with ® are registered in the United States Patent
and Trademark Office, the Canadian Trade Marks Office and in other
countries.

Visit Silhouette at www.eHarlequin.com

Printed in U.S.A.

Books by Amy J. Fetzer

Silhouette Desire

Anybody's Dad #1089
The Unlikely Bodyguard #1132
The Re-Enlisted Groom #1181
*Going...Going...Wed! #1265
*Wife for Hire #1305
*Taming the Beast #1361
*Having His Child #1383
*Single Father Seeks... #1445
The SEAL's Surprise Baby #1467
Awakening Beauty #1548

Harlequin Intrigue

Under His Protection #733

*Wife, Inc.

AMY J. FETZER

was born in New England and raised all over the world. She uses her own experiences in creating the characters and settings for her novels. Married more than twenty years to a United States Marine and the mother of two sons, Amy covets the moments when she can curl up with a cup of cappuccino and a good book.

For the
R.H.S. Southern Pearls

With whom secrets are sacred
Fun is learning to be *really* lazy
And dessert before dinner takes on new meaning.

I love y'all.

One

It was moments like these that made Lane Douglas glad she'd changed her name. Elaina Honora Giovanni didn't get involved with the police. Police reports meant giving your ID and putting the incident on the blotter, and that was open season for the press.

There was one particular member of the press corps out there just waiting to read her name somewhere and come hunting like a wolf for its prey.

And something as simple as a car accident would be enough to lead him right to her.

When the sound of screeching tires, splashing water and a loud solid crunch had registered, Lane knew before she whipped around that her car was the victim.

Attacked by a low-slung, silver sports car.

The impact popped open the trunk of her car.

"*Buona fortuna* as usual, Elaina," she muttered to herself, dropping a box full of books on the porch of her shop, then rushing down the steps to the curb. Cold winter rain soaked through her clothes, matted her hair.

She could feel the tightly twisted bun on the top of her head sagging already.

Never good in a crisis, she looked first at the books in the trunk, then at the man still behind the wheel of his car. His loud cursing told her that he at least was uninjured. The car door opened and he climbed out, glaring at the damage before meeting her gaze.

"Are you all right?" he asked, and whipped out a cell phone.

"Fine, fine. I wasn't in the car, remember? Are you okay?" she shouted over the rain.

"Yes, dammit." He kicked the tire, then winced.

"Smart move," she said.

He smiled at her, tipping the phone away for a second. "Tyler. Tyler McKay."

She knew who he was. It was hard to live in Bradford, South Carolina, and not know the McKays. Rich, handsome and eligible didn't begin to describe Tyler. With dark hair and light-blue eyes, he was the most noticed man in town. And that wasn't even counting that long, lean body in a leather jacket and jeans.

She swung her gaze to their cars.

His hadn't fared well against hers.

The sports car looked like an accordion halfway through a song.

Then she noticed the rain pouring over the crushed

metal of her trunk like a stream over rocks and dribbling onto the carton of books.

"Oh, no, my stock!"

He barely glanced at it, still talking into the phone. Then he closed the cell phone and observed, "They're ruined."

She glared at him. "Yes, thank you for pointing that out. What was your first clue?" She tried shutting the trunk, but the twisted metal refused to oblige.

He took off his jacket and like Sir Walter Raleigh, covered the books. "How's that?"

"A Band-Aid to a bleeding head wound."

"Gallantry is never appreciated."

"Perhaps when it's sincere it would be." She threw off his jacket and lifted out a soaked carton of books.

He picked up the other carton and walked behind her. "The cops will be here in a couple of minutes."

He probably pulled someone's chain for that quick service. When your family owned practically half the town, it wasn't hard. "Good." She unlocked the shop door and pushed inside.

"Look. It's my fault."

She paused at the doorway to look back at him. It was a mistake. He was too close, his front to her back, and she got a full dose of him in one flash. Vivid blue eyes pinned her, as if the chance to look at her would be snatched away any second and he needed to get in a good stare while he could. The little crinkles at the corners of his eyes spoke of countless smiles, and rainwater dripped off his dark hair onto his leather jacket.

When she caught a whiff of his warm woodsy cologne, Lane wanted to inhale deeply. Instead, she said, "The rain, the curve off Bay street and a slick road are to blame."

He grinned. "Does this mean I'm forgiven?" he said softly.

That smile lit something inside her and made her pulse jump hard. Her chilled skin was suddenly warmer, and ignoring the way she reacted to him wasn't as easy as she expected. He probably knew exactly the effect he had on a person. "Do you need my forgiveness?"

"No, but I'd like to have it. Being neighborly and all."

That smile came again and she hurried into the shop and set the box on the counter before looking at him again.

"Then, yes, you're forgiven. But I reserve the right to needle you." She smoothed her hair back off her face. Her glasses steamed up and slid down her nose. "Although since I didn't put any change in the parking meter, with my luck *I'll* be getting the ticket."

"You won't. I promise."

She arched a brow. "Falling on your sword for me? Now that's gallantry."

He smiled and Lane felt her insides shift and bow. This was so not good, she thought.

"And your name is?" he asked.

"Lane Douglas." It tripped easily off her tongue after nearly two years, she thought. Sad that lying about who she was had become second nature. He held out his hand. She shook it once, quickly, then jerked back. Okay, so his skin was delightfully

3 1833 04500 8296

warm, and though she might have expected smooth and pampered, it wasn't. She'd felt at least one callus. He probably got that golfing.

She turned her back to him, inspecting her sodden books and mentally calculating the cost to replace them.

"Nice place," he said. "Is it new?"

"It's been here for 150 years, Mr. McKay," she said, although she knew he meant newly remodeled.

"Call me Tyler, please. Mr. McKay is my dad."

She hunted in her purse. "I don't want to get that personal. I may have to sue."

His gaze narrowed. "I will make full restitution, Miss Douglas."

She faced him, holding out her driver's license and insurance card. "Good. Why don't you hail the cops?" She nodded to the windows. The blue lights of the police car flashed against the watery glass.

Tyler stared at her for a second, then, with a sharp nod, took her information and stepped out onto the covered porch. She wasn't worried about the police, for Lane Douglas had nothing to hide. While he talked to the officers, Lane tried to salvage the books, but there really was no hope. A water-damage sale was in order, and she'd just cut her losses as usual.

Like she'd done with her family.

Stay a Giovanni and live in a cage. Become Lane Douglas and live like a normal human being.

Hmm.

Tough choice.

Heiress to a winery or not.

Now if she could just get Tyler McKay out of her store without piquing his curiosity, she'd be fine.

She'd spent the past year avoiding McKay—and anyone else in his family. There were quite a few, and they attracted the attention of the media like the Kennedys. And like the Giovannis. Tyler McKay was wealthy enough, affluent enough, to have traveled in the same social circles as her family. Not to mention that her face had once been plastered over every newspaper and tabloid in the country, and someone might recognize her.

Her identity had to stay a secret.

With the exception of her father, even her own family didn't know where she was. She'd do just about anything to keep it that way.

The woman couldn't be more chilling, Tyler thought, glancing back into the shop as the deputy filled out the report. She was rummaging in a box of books, and his gaze traveled from the round glasses and the reddish-brown hair falling out of its tight bun and drooping onto the collar of her sweater to her skirt, wet and hanging to ankles, hidden by what looked like combat boots.

She reminded him of a spinster schoolteacher, but there was something about her that was far from spinsterish. He couldn't put his finger on it yet, but she had incredible eyes, deep-set, long-lashed and the color of Irish whiskey that those glasses couldn't shield.

She was reserved, businesslike, but he had the feeling she was trying too hard. Tyler had never seen her before, which was strange. He'd thought he knew everyone in Bradford.

"I need to speak to Miss Douglas," the cop said.

Tyler nodded and they stepped back inside. Cold rain turned the sky a little darker gray and dreary, but inside the house-turned-bookshop, it was warm and smelled like cinnamon. She wasn't visible now, and he called her name.

She appeared from the back of the store with a tray of steaming coffee and cups.

"To take the chill off." Lane told herself she didn't have to invite friendship or anything, but she didn't have to be rude to McKay. He knew everyone and everyone read books. So it was good for business.

Tyler took a cup, warming his hands.

The cop declined, asked her a few questions, then handed them each a copy of the report and left. Tyler tucked his copy in his jacket and sipped coffee.

Lane wished he would leave, too. The man unnerved her, and if the FBI's constant questions about what she knew about her brother Angel's alleged illegal business deals hadn't done that, it was saying something. She'd just as soon not listen.

"How come I haven't seen you around before?"

"Well, I sell books. Do you read?"

"Of course I do."

A smile teased her lips and she peered at him through the round glasses. Tyler was struck again by the beauty of her eyes.

"Apparently not enough, Mr. McKay."

Tyler grinned. "You're still upset about the car."

"No, not really," she said. "Maybe I can get a new one out of it." He liked the little smile she was trying not to show.

"It would have to be totaled for that."

"Well, I could leave it there, and if you go driving again, that shouldn't be a problem."

He laughed, a soft rumble that matched the thunder outside. Just then the little bell above the door tinkled as a boy of about twelve entered the shop, shaking off the rain. Lane smiled at him.

"Man, what a downpour," he said. "Hey, Mr. McKay."

"Hi, Davis."

The kid frowned out the window, inclining his head. "Is that your car all smashed up out there?"

"Sadly, yes."

"Aw, man, that's an insult to a car like that."

"It can be fixed."

Lane glanced between the two. "Can I help you with something?"

The boy held up a plastic packet of flyers. "Winter Festival flyers. Can I put one in your window?"

"Sure."

Setting down her cup, she crossed to the boy, gathering tape and a small towel as she went. She handed him the towel to dry his face and chatted softly with him as she put the flyer in the front window, asking him if the location was what he needed.

Tyler saw a different woman just then, one with kinder eyes than she'd had for him. He didn't get it. There weren't many women who could resist the McKay charm. Or so his mother told him. And he was turning his on high.

"See ya later, Mr. McKay."

"Later, Davis."

"Watch the traffic," Lane said. "There are some reckless drivers out there."

"Being the graceful victor is out of the question, huh?" Tyler said after the boy left.

"It's not every day the town playboy slams into my poor defenseless car."

"You forgave me, and who said I was a playboy?"

She let out a long-suffering sigh and walked behind the counter. "Who hasn't, McKay?" She slid an extra flyer in front of her, reading the list of events and ignoring him. Which was next to impossible.

"Lies, I swear."

Lane looked up. He was smiling, and she thought, he's dangerous, get him out of here. "You needn't defend yourself. I form my own opinions and though I know who you are, I don't care what you do."

"Intriguing," he said. "A woman who doesn't care what gossips have to say?"

She lifted her gaze, looking at him over the rim of her glasses. What did he know about gossips? A few locals musing about his love life? Hah. He should try life in the big leagues. When people in Outer Mongolia knew what you had for breakfast or what you wore to bed. Now that took gossip to a whole new level. And put it on the front page of a tabloid that every person in America who goes through a checkout line at the grocery store can see.

Oh, yeah. There was gossip and then there was *gossip*.

"Isn't there someplace you should be?" she asked, anxious to get him out of her shop, out of her life. "Like work?"

Tyler felt something in him pitch by just looking into her eyes. She could probably give a man frostbite without even trying. And yet, something told him, it might be worth it just to see if he could start a fire in solid ice. "Nope."

"Ahh, the life of Riley."

"It's raining," he reminded her. "You won't get many customers today."

"You'd be surprised what people will do for a good book on a day like this. It's perfect curl-up-and-read weather."

He wouldn't mind curling up right here. The stray thought surprised him and he blinked as if to catch it back. After all, she with her waterlogged-librarian look wasn't exactly the stuff of dreams. But still... those whiskey eyes of hers continued to draw him in. Whether he wanted to be or not.

"Are you working the festival?" He pointed to the flyer she'd taken from the boy and was taping to her counter.

"No."

Now that surprised him. The Winter Festival was the one time a year when every merchant in Bradford banded together. Good for the town, good for business. Plus, it was a hell of a lot of fun, with different events scheduled every day for a couple of weeks. People came from all over the state for it. "How come?"

"I chose not to."

"Party pooper."

She was trying not to smile again. He could tell.

"All the local businesses join in," he said.

She arched a brow, still looking over the rims of her glasses. "The gas station does? The carwash?"

"You bet. Dennis at the gas station gives away

tickets for a free carwash with every fill-up. And Mike at the carwash gives away ten dollars worth of gas with every wash and wax." He took another sip of coffee and rocked back on his heels. "So how about it?"

"I sell books and I don't do it from a vendor's cart."

"You sell coffee, too." He gestured to the small coffee bar surrounded by cozy overstuffed chairs.

"Oh, sure, big contribution—mocha lattes."

"On a cold afternoon, sure. Why don't you give it a try?"

"Who are you, the mayor?" she asked, shaking her head and smiling.

"Hmm." He pretended to give that some thought. "Mayor McKay. Kinda like the sound of that."

"Uh-huh. Why don't you go to work, make more money?" She took the coffee cup from him midsip and set it behind the counter.

He blinked. "You show all your customers that charm?"

"I save it for the really big spenders."

Tyler's lips twitched. He loved her sense of humor. "You'll go under in a month with that attitude."

She scoffed. "I've been here over a year, McKay, and survived just fine."

"Ah, but is surviving ever really enough?" he asked.

She gave him a look that said he'd just stepped into too-personal ground. "You don't have to hang around, McKay. You've done your civic duty."

"Hey, is it me you don't like or the McKay name?"

The McKays. Wealthy, privileged. And he stood here thinking she was a struggling businesswoman. It was on the tip of her tongue to tell him that she knew what life was like with unlimited funds. What it was like to be the talk of not only the town, but on two continents. Giovanni Wines. Suspected Mafia ties of money laundering, her sibling's picture in the paper with some questionable businessmen. Then there was the sublime thrill of seeing her own face on the cover of a tabloid—and her career as a clothing designer ruined. All because reporter Dan Jacobs had said he loved her when he really only wanted to use her to get an "inside" story on her family. The worst part was that she'd loved him, and he'd used it to betray her.

She stared at the floor, her chest suddenly tight as a drum, as she pushed at the hurt still wedged in her heart. She had closed herself off because people she'd loved had lied. People hurt you, and didn't care how much if they got what they wanted. People like Dan Jacobs.

Books, on the other hand, never wounded you so hard that you didn't think you could ever get back up.

Books took you away...

"Miss Douglas?"

She looked up, forcing a smile.

Tyler frowned, wondering where she'd gone just then. "You okay?"

Her expression changed from brooding to falsely cheerful, and all it did was heighten his awareness of her. Which was bordering on overload. She had a regal quality about her, not arrogant, but dignified and sophisticated. And even the librarian clothes and glasses didn't hide it from him.

"At the risk of sounding redundant, I'm fine."

Tyler didn't get the cold shoulder from women often, and he admitted it rattled him. It was suddenly a challenge to get a real smile out of her.

When he continued to stare, she said, "Shouldn't you be calling a wrecker? Calling your office or your girlfriend?"

No, he thought, no girlfriend, or at least no one steady. Right now, he was having fun doing the love-'em-and-leave-'em-graciously game. Because not so long ago, he'd come damn close to saying "I do" to the wrong woman. A woman who'd wanted the McKay money, but not the man.

It had been two years and though it didn't hurt anymore, the memory of how blind he'd been still stung. And the sudden flash reminded him that he would never know if a woman wanted him or a key to his family's fortune.

"No girlfriend to call, thanks for asking. And I called the wrecker when I was talking to the deputy." He tipped his head a bit and leaned on the counter, closing the space between them. "You're real hot to get me out of here, aren't you. Why is that?"

Lane kept right where she was, refusing to back off. It wasn't a smart move. He smelled wonderful. Warm and spicy. And the brown leather jacket and tan shirt made him look downright yummy. She sucked in a breath that unfortunately brought his scent down deep inside her. "Unlike the idle rich, I have a business to run."

Her voice was like smoke, low and throaty, and Tyler tried placing her accent. Not Southern for sure, but the region wasn't definite, and it sounded slightly European sometimes.

"Mr. McKay?"

"Yes?"

"I believe your pocket is ringing."

He blinked and reached for his cell phone.

"Fan club?" Lane asked.

He winked at her and her insides did a dance she'd almost forgotten. "Hello, Mom, yes, I'm fine."

Lane smothered a laugh.

"Good grief, how did you hear about this so soon?" A pause and then he said, "Tell Mrs. Ashbury I'm fine. Yes, yes, I will on my way home." He closed the phone. "I have to give her proof I'm not lying on a stretcher with my head split open."

"I could accommodate you if you want some sympathy?" She hefted a resin statue of a gnome reading a book, her lips twitching with a smile.

"I'll pass." He chuckled and stepped away before she gave in to the urge to bean him. "Send me the bill for the books," he said as he strode to the door.

"I will."

"Or better yet, I'll stop by tomorrow and pick it up." Tyler somehow knew that would get her riled.

"The U.S. postal system is fine, Mr. McKay. It works for most people."

Half out the door, Tyler grinned back at her. "I'm not most people, Miss Douglas."

He shut the door and trotted down the steps, hailing a cab and leaving behind his wrecked car.

And Lane felt as if she'd just been warned. This wasn't the end for Tyler McKay. And that, for her, was dangerous.

Two

Tyler leaned against the kitchen counter in his parents' house and bit into a sandwich. Since the accident hadn't left him bleeding on the side of the road, his mom allowed him to snitch it from her kitchen.

Good thing, because his own fridge didn't have anything in it that wasn't growing fuzz. He really should remember to shop and then actually stay home long enough to eat it.

"I can't believe that you haven't been in that bookstore before today." His mother poured herself some hot tea.

"Have you?"

"Once, with Diana."

His mother and her friend Diana Ashbury had known each other since they were in high school and were as close now as they'd been then. Tyler had grown up with Diana's children and her son, Jace, was a good friend of his.

"So...what did you think of the owner. Diana shops there all the time. She adores Miss Douglas."

"Adores?" Tyler almost choked on a sip of soda. He couldn't imagine anyone *adoring* the Lane he knew. The woman was witty, yes, but she was very cool. And she had eyes that said, "Don't even think about it," and that just made him *want* to think about it.

"Oh, yes, Di says she can find any book and doesn't charge extra for getting it."

That was good business sense and Tyler appreciated that. Too bad Lane didn't spend more effort on charm. Then again, maybe it was just him she didn't like. "She isn't participating in the Winter Festival."

His mother looked up from stirring her tea. "Oh? How come?"

Tyler finished off the sandwich, and when he grabbed a dish towel to wipe his mouth, his mother tossed him a napkin and muttered, "I swear, Tyler McKay, your manners are terrible sometimes. I know I taught you better."

"You did. Sorry." He gave her a sheepish grin. "I don't know why she's not joining in. I got the feeling she just wanted to be left alone."

"Well, she's fairly new to town and she should meet the other shopkeepers. Everyone talks about what a wonderful job she did restoring that house. And as a member of the historical society, I'm delighted. If she hadn't restored it, the town council would have torn down that lovely old place."

Tyler admitted the two-story house did look spectacular. Painted soft yellow with green shutters and door, it had a white wraparound porch with some curly fretwork in the eaves. But what killed him was that he hadn't noticed it until today.

Had he had his face that deep in work not to see the simple things going on around him? He'd been working long hours lately. Getting McKay Enterprises into the big-league competition with larger construction companies had been his father's dream before he died. His father had taken the business regional last year, and in another year Tyler would take the company statewide.

"Yes, I agree Ms. Douglas should join in," his mother said, breaking into his thoughts. "Perhaps I'll ask her myself. Diana is the festival chairperson, you know."

"When is she not?" His mother and her friend headed nearly every committee that existed in Bradford, South Carolina.

"I'd rather you two didn't march over there and instigate something." Lane would blame him for it, he thought.

"Really? Why?" When he didn't jump in with a response, his mother eyed him for a second, then her face lit up.

Oh, man.

Before he could stop her, she blurted, "You're attracted to her!"

"No, of course not. Well, maybe. It's hard to say." Heck. He rubbed his face for a second. It was plain strange. Lane was definitely not his type, whatever his type was. But this was something he sure didn't want to speculate about with his mother. "I don't know her at all, but she doesn't let anyone get close, that's for sure.''

"Anyone—or you?''

Tyler hadn't seen her with anyone else but Davis and to the kid she was kind. But to *him*...well, she'd practically kicked him out the door. "Me.''

"Oh, nonsense. You're making assumptions, Tyler. You just met her. And let's remember, you met her after wrecking her car. Not exactly the best first impression, son. But as I recall, she isn't like the women I've seen you date before.''

"It wouldn't matter. I'm not looking for a wife, so get that gleam out of your eye, okay?''

His mom made a face. "Clarice was never the woman for you. Can't you get beyond it?''

"No, and you liked her.'' It sounded like an accusation, even to him.

His mother frowned distastefully. "I tolerated her because you loved her.''

Well, this was news. "Good grief, Mom, why didn't you say anything before?''

"It's a mother's duty to accept and love the woman her son loves.''

There was no doubt in his mind that she believed that bunk. And no doubt she'd meant well. "In the future, I'd like to hear your opinion.''

She blinked, obviously taken aback. "Why?''

"Because you're a good judge of character, and besides, it might have saved me the humiliation of learning the truth when I did.''

The week of his wedding. Literally just hours before people were getting on planes to come witness the event. He'd been at a party that some friends were giving them when he heard Clarice say to one of her bridesmaids that she could "put up with anything, even him, for McKay money." Tyler had ended his engagement in the middle of the party, taken back his grandmother's ring and left on his honeymoon trip, alone. It still hadn't been easy coming back to gossip. And he hadn't told a soul what had happened except his best man—his brother Kyle—and his parents. They had a right to know the truth, but no one else.

He hadn't cared what Clarice had told anyone. He'd heard enough of her lies to last an eternity, and he wasn't rising to the bait to defend himself, either. As far as he was concerned, the door was closed on that part of his life. He wasn't about to repeat the mistake by opening it again. Ever.

"It's been nearly three years, Tyler."

"Who's counting? I'm enjoying myself, Mom, so leave it alone," he said, then kissed the top of her head and was out the door before she had a chance to hunt him down and reopen the wound.

And just the reminder of that staggering humiliation told him he couldn't trust his own judgment. Especially when his heart was in for the ride.

Lane curled up in an overstuffed chair, setting the teacup on the end table and wrapping herself in an afghan she didn't really need. It was a process, she thought, preparing for a ritual evening of reading. Tea, blanket, soft lights and music. The scent of cinnamon cookies on the plate beside her teacup from the bakery next door. Simple pleasures.

She'd never had rituals before moving to Bradford.

Never thought she wanted them, never thought how lonely she was, only how alone she wanted to be. In her old life she'd be getting ready for a late dinner and the theater. And turning away from flashbulbs, and microphones shoved in her face.

She shivered and pulled the afghan closer. Her apartment, above the bookshop, had four rooms with a small kitchen. Another kitchen was still downstairs, and she'd had its old breakfast area retooled for moments just like this. A place out of the store traffic where her customers could curl up and read for a bit, chat with friends, discuss a new book.

A small sound broke the silence.

She glanced over her shoulder toward her bedroom. "Hello, Ramses. Too wet outside to prowl?"

The coal-black cat purred, prancing toward her, then paused to rub his cheek against her foot. Satisfied that Lane knew he was gracing her with his presence, the cat lowered his bulk on the braided rug.

The phone rang, startling her. She blinked at it, thinking it might be her father calling to badger her again. At last she answered it.

"Hello, Lane."

Tyler McKay. He was the last person she'd expected to call. "This is a private number. How did you get it? I should sue the phone company."

"Can't. I got your number from Diana Ashbury."

"I'll have to overcharge her for the next batch of books she buys."

He laughed.

"What do you want, Mr. McKay?"

"First, for you to call me Tyler."

"Will that make you go away?"

"Can't bet on it. I'm calling to ask if you'll help with some community service."

"And what service might that be?"

"The children's pageant."

"Oh, no." Lane shook her head as if he could see her. "I've never worked with children. Besides, I have no talent to contribute."

"Come on, you can swing a hammer."

"You mean at an actual nail?"

He laughed softly, it was an intimate sound, and for a second she wondered if he was in bed. "I love it when you talk tools."

"You're pathetic." But the smile she wore was starting to hurt.

"What are you wearing?" he asked.

"Excuse me?"

"Do you wear those ugly boots in your house?"

"No, they're sitting on the back steps standing guard against the fashion police. They're outlaws, you know."

His chuckle melted through her blood, and she curled more deeply into the chair.

"Let me guess—you're wearing flannel up to your throat."

Lane looked down at the satin chemise and matching blood-red robe. "Yes, with little flowers on it and a pink bow. And they're footie pajamas too. Now the point of this conversation is…?"

"Curiosity."

"It killed the cat." Ramses whined at her feet. "Sorry."

"Are you talking to me?"

"No, to my cat, Ramses."

"Why Ramses?"

"Because the Pharaohs worshipped cats and they have never let us forget it."

His laughter was a quick short burst that made her smile.

"A woman with cats and flannel living alone has potential for a lonely life, Lane."

"I guess I'm doomed, then. Should I break out the doilies?"

He chuckled again and Lane felt the sound coat her. "Not quite yet."

"Why do you care?" she asked.

"You're too sexy to be locked away."

She blinked, looking down at her cat and mouthing "Sexy?" Only Tyler McKay would think combat boots and long drab skirts were meant to entice a man when they were meant to play down her looks and hide her identity.

"Do you need glasses?"

"I see fine…and I like what I see."

She felt herself flush with excitement. "Good night."

"No, it's good night, *Tyler,*" he said patiently. "Say it. It won't make you go up in flames."

Feeling playful, she said in her sexiest throaty voice, "Good night, Tyler," then hung up.

Torture goes both ways, she thought, and knew that would probably get her into the very trouble she was trying to avoid. Just the same, her insides were tickled, and she realized he was on some quest to learn more about her. While she was flattered beyond belief, she couldn't let him that close.

If anyone learned who she really was, her neat little life would be over.

Lane glanced up as a customer came through the door. She recognized the designer suit—the Italian-milled fabric, the exceptional fit—before the woman in her recognized the man wearing it.

Okay, she was impressed, and she had to swallow to keep her jaw from dropping to the counter. Tyler McKay could have been one of her runway models at her design shows, he looked that good. A thought she was definitely keeping to herself.

"Is this proof you work for a living, or are you playing dress-up?" she said, gesturing at the suit. His crisp white shirt, she could tell, was an exquisite silk-and-cotton blend, and her fingers almost itched to inspect the seams and facings.

"I'm between appointments."

He stopped at the counter, and Lane remembered the sound of his voice late last night. Soft and deep, wrapping around her and dragging her down. After the call, she couldn't even concentrate on her book.

"What are you doing here again?"

"I brought your car." He pointed out the window at the black vehicle sitting at the curb.

"That's not my car, Mr. McKay."

"I know. Yours was nearly an antique, and it'll take a while to get parts. This is a loaner."

It was black SUV. One of the smaller models and it looked brand-new.

"My insurance offers a loaner."

"So does mine," he said. "That's it."

"I don't think so."

"Look, I'm at fault. My insurance pays."

"That's a McKay Enterprises car. I've seen them."

"It might look like one, but it's not." He studied her for a second longer than she wanted. "You're spoiling for an argument, aren't you?"

"Yes. Can't you tell by my tone?"

"If I knew you better..."

She gave him a thin look that said it wasn't going to happen.

"Okay, stay a stranger, but you still need a car." He dangled the keys.

"I have one and as soon as it's repaired, I'll—"

"—still have a piece of junk."

Her chin tipped up, her lips twitching. "I like to think I've been driving cars with character."

"That one was a bad seed, trust me. It's time you made better friends."

Her pride reared. "Do you dictate to everyone or just me?"

"If I thought I could, I'd try harder to get you to join the festival."

Another thin look. "Don't get off the subject," she warned. "I don't need your car or your money, McKay. I don't want it, in fact."

Tyler grinned. Big. And Lane felt her heart skip all the way to her throat and shiver with pleasure for a couple seconds. It made her light-headed. When was the last time she met anyone who smiled so much? Who was just plain happy with life?

Oh, gee, said a voice in her head. Doesn't the fact that he's worth millions have something to do with that? He didn't have much to worry about, did he?

Money made people strange. But from her experience, it didn't generate an attitude like his. Which she was still trying to figure out. Why was he flirting with her? Or was he just testing his charm on the homely girl? In her present lackluster state of dress, hair and makeup, she knew she wasn't attractive. It was intentional. A goal to blend into the woodwork and not be noticed. The less recognizable she was, the better.

She'd been a designer with her own couture showrooms in Paris and Milan. She knew what clothing flattered, what hid, what exposed. Now she chose not to expose anything, using the wrong colors and styles, and wearing her normally short hair longer and whipped tight to her head. She wore glasses because she needed them, and she had a darling trendy pair upstairs in her apartment. Yet when she was in public, she wore round, plain, tortoiseshell glasses. They were too large for her face and the color of her eyes. Another good shield to hide behind.

"I've come to ask for community service again."

"My store is my community service."

"But the children," he said, pouring a little whine into his voice.

Inside, she was cracking up over this guy. He made her want to smile, but he'd take the smile as encouragement. "That's unfair."

He shrugged. "I use what I can."

"The last time I was with a child, I was one. Besides, the kids have parents to volunteer. PTA, bake sales. I really have nothing to offer." It was sad but true. A couture designer wouldn't be much good in a pie-baking contest.

The bell over the door tinkled and a woman stepped inside. She paused at the entrance, which was the foyer of the old house, and looked around. Inspecting a bit, Lane decided. She was slim and petite, her silver hair cut to perfection in a sleek bob. Her clothes, the next thing Lane focused on, were classic. Camel cashmere slacks and a navy blouse with a camel wool jacket. She'd draped a printed scarf over her shoulder and across her chest, secured with a small glittering pin. Elegant, Lane thought as the woman moved forward.

She stopped beside Tyler, and from Lane's perspective, he seemed to loom over the woman.

"Hello, Mother," he said in a tone tinged with annoyance. "Didn't our discussion yesterday mean anything?"

"You dictated, I didn't listen. I'm your mother, I'm allowed." She gave him a backhanded smack in the middle of his chest. "Introduce us."

Lane's gaze shot to Tyler as she moved out from behind the counter. "Welcome, Mrs. McKay. I'm Lane Douglas. It's a pleasure to meet you. Diana Ashbury talks of you often."

"It's a pleasure, dear. And call me Laura. I popped in once with Diana a while back. She loves your store."

"She hides in the corner with a cup of coffee and the latest thriller."

"I think she comes for the cappuccino and quiet more than the books."

Lane offered them coffee, crossing into the old living-room area to make it. While she prepared the coffee, the noise from the steam pressure drowned out whatever Tyler and his mother were saying. A quick glance caught Tyler's scowl and his mom shooing him off.

Mother and son approached the counter, still talking. About her.

"I was trying to convince Lane to join the festival, and seeing as that won't work…yet, I'm trying to settle for help with the pageant."

Lane glared over the counter at him. "So you brought out the big guns?"

He glanced briefly at his mother. "I knew it would be a heavy battle."

"Have you no manners? No means no, McKay."

"My mother was just commenting on my manners the other day." He winked at his mom. "Must have been those college years out from under her iron thumb."

"Tyler, behave."

"Yes, ma'am."

Lane had to smile. At least someone could get him to back down.

"We could really use extra help," Laura McKay said.

"She thinks that's what parents are for."

Lane pinned Tyler with a hard look. "I can speak for myself, thank you." She looked at Laura as she came around the edge of the cappuccino bar with two froth-filled mugs. "I hope you understand that I really don't want to spread myself so thin when I've just opened the store this year and I'm running it alone."

Laura sipped her cappuccino, licking froth from her lip. "This is fabulous. No wonder Di takes refuge in here.'' She set the cup down and looked at Lane. ''I can understand that your business comes first. It should. However—'' she paused, giving Lane a sweet smile ''—we just need a few extra pairs of hands. The parents are helping as much as they can, and Tyler is in charge of making the sets.''

Lane's gaze slid to his. ''Volunteered or arm twisted?''

''A little of both,'' he said, lifting his cup and licking the froth off the top.

Lane watched him, biting the inside of her mouth and wondering if he knew what she was thinking, feeling. One look in his eyes said, oh yeah. Every womanly instinct to outright flirt with this man screamed through her, telling her to get close enough to learn if that smiling mouth tasted as good as it looked. Another part of her brain was busy reminding her that she was alone for a reason. Another man had wanted something from her and hid it under the guise of friendship, then love.

Now there was Tyler. And people wanted her to work with him?

As if he knew her thoughts, his eyes darkened and seared her with a strange heat. Oh, so not good.

''Please, Lane,'' Laura said softly. ''The way you've decorated this house proves you have talent for design.''

''Thank you. It's a hobby.'' Lane almost choked. She hated lying, especially to this nice woman. She felt herself caving in. It was as if she had to pay for the lie, although the lie was to protect her.

Now that was twisted.

She surrendered to the guilt. "How long would you need me?"

Laura smiled again, pleased. "Just a couple of hours in the evening. The festival starts next week and we must be finished in time for the opening children's show and play."

"All right. A couple of hours after I close up shop for the night." She ignored the grin spreading across Tyler's face. "Do I need to bring anything?"

"No, the local businesses have contributed materials. Say seven o'clock at the theater?"

Lane agreed.

Laura said a quick goodbye and was out the door. Tyler stayed behind. Picking up his coffee again, he said, "The first session is tonight."

"A promise is a promise, McKay. I'll be there."

He looked at his watch.

"You have to go? What a shame," she said. "Take that car when you leave." When she reached for his mug, Tyler latched onto her wrist.

Lane felt warmth burn through her skin to her blood. He let go, sliding his hand under the sleeve of her sweater and pulled her near.

Lane's heart did a wild dance and she could barely swallow. "McKay."

"Your skin is so soft," he said.

"Good lotion." His fingers played over her bare skin, and it was silly, it was just her arm, but Lane felt as if they were playing somewhere else entirely. And if he didn't stop, she was going to yank him into the back room and try a kiss on for size.

He searched her gaze. "I don't know what it is

about you that's driving me nuts, Lane Douglas, but I'm willing to wait to find out.''

''There's nothing to learn, so it'll be a long wait.''

He leaned closer, tipping his head, and Lane thought, *Come on, kiss me.*

''I'm a Southern boy.'' She felt his warm breath on her lips. ''We're long on patience.''

''Tell that to the back end of my car.''

The alarm on his watch went off, and he clucked his tongue and eased back. He stared at her for a second longer, then releasing a heavy sigh, made an about-face and headed to the door. She looked down and saw the car keys on the counter.

''McKay, take these keys.''

He ignored her and reached for the knob.

''Tyler!''

He flashed her a look over his shoulder that said triumph. Then he was out the door and sliding into a matching black SUV.

''Talking to that man is like talking to wood,'' she muttered, then picked up the keys. They were still warm from handling. She pocketed them and did what she did best. Ignored them. Ignored him.

It lasted all of ten seconds, and she dropped into a chair, plucking at her clothes and letting the build-up of steam in her system escape.

Oh, yes, that man.

Definitely dangerous.

Because Lane knew that she could fall for him, and there would be no getting back up this time.

Three

The lights in the town theater were almost blinding. Adults and children were scattered across the stage and the wide area meant for the orchestra, each small group working on different projects.

Lane had made her way down to near the stage when Tyler came through the outer doors, carrying a stack of two-by-fours on his shoulder. He stopped short when he saw her, and a grin spread across his handsome face, warming her right down to her toes. His gaze dropped to her boots and he made a face, shaking his head. She stuck out her tongue at him.

"I knew you'd show."

"Don't gloat, McKay. I knuckled under matriarchal pressure, nothing more."

"Good to know something gets to you."

You do, she thought when he gave her a long,

heated look that said more than she wanted. Why was he so interested in her? She'd have to check her appearance, dowdy it up a bit more, she thought, watching him trot off. Well, more specifically, she watched his behind in tight, worn jeans, the toolbelt rocking low on his hips.

Lane found the chairperson, Diana Ashbury, easily. The woman was short and dark-haired, with a porcelain complexion that reminded Lane of her own mother's. Lionetta Giovanni, of course, wouldn't be caught dead volunteering for a children's pageant. She'd much rather throw money at a charity so she could attend the parties in one of her daughter's designs. Diana, on the other hand, was hip-deep in coordinating tasks, wearing jeans and a sweatshirt, both covered by an apron bulging with craft supplies.

"Thanks for coming, Lane."

"Two hands, ready and willing," Lane said.

Diana blew out a short breath and waved at the stations positioned all over the theater. "Pick a job," Diana said, then scanned her notes on a clipboard.

"Put me where I'm needed most," she told the woman.

"We don't have costumes even remotely finished." Diana's voice held a little bit of plea.

Costumes? A long-buried corner of Lane's heart leaped to life. Sewing. Maybe some designing. It wouldn't be couture, but she could design clothing again. Even if it was for a children's play. She tried to disguise the eagerness in her voice when she said, "Say no more. I'm on it."

Lane headed to the orchestra pit where a large table was set up with a sewing machine at each end,

manned by two young women. Yards of bright felt,
fabric and trims were scattered over the table and
nearby chairs. A half-dozen children raced around
the aisles, while two little girls sat in the middle of
the floor, their heads together, oblivious to everything but the dolls they played with. Between stitch-
ing and cutting, the moms hollered for the kids to
calm down. Lane introduced herself to the two
women, Suzanne and Marcy.

"Why don't you both take a break and let me
handle the sewing?" Lane said.

"You sure?" Suzanne clipped a thread as Marcy
spotted a small child climbing onto the stage, where
men were wielding dangerous saws and drills. Lane
nodded and both women shot after the children.

Costumes were something Lane could do without
thinking. She quickly organized the mess at the long
table, checking fabric length and yardage against
necessary colors and trims. After a quick glance
through the patterns, she slid into the chair at the
machine. The noise of hammers and kids, of adult
chatter and the whine of drills didn't penetrate her
concentration.

When she looked up to call for Anna, the pageant's fairy princess, Tyler was staring down at her
from the stage. He had his hand on his hip, the other
twirling a hammer like a six-shooter.

Her heart sped up, and she felt herself blush like
a teenager. Then her stomach clenched in a tight
knot. Oh, the man had power, she thought. It didn't
hurt that he was wearing a blue cable sweater that
made his eyes look deeper, and jeans that molded to
every feature from the waist down.

"I was wondering if you were coming up for air."

Lane glanced at her watch and realized she'd been at this for an hour already.

"You were not."

His smile faded a bit and his gaze narrowed. "I never lie, Lane."

He looked angry all of a sudden, she thought, and her own lies struck her like the hammer he held. She had good reasons for hiding, she reasoned. For lying.

"I'll remember that." And remember that he wouldn't tolerate that she was lying to him, she thought, reaffirming her decision to keep her distance.

"Will you be my date for the Winter Ball?"

She blinked at the abrupt shift in the conversation and couldn't help but notice that a couple of people stopped what they were doing and stared.

"The what?" She'd heard him. She was just stalling. Needed time to think.

"The Winter Ball is the last event of the festival. Big bash, catered, at the country club."

"I see." She took a deep breath and ignored the piece of her that wanted to say yes. Instead, she simply said, "No, thank you."

He let out a sigh. Clearly he'd expected that reaction. "Then I'll settle for you having dinner with me." He squatted at the edge of the stage, looming over her.

"No, thank you again." She tore her gaze from him and called to Anna. The girl raced over and Lane took her hand, then looked at Tyler. "Excuse us, the princess has a fitting."

"You have to eat," he called.

"Not with you."

His short laugh flowed down from the stage. He went back to his job, and Lane had to drag her attention to the girl. Once she did, she got caught up in little Anna's excitement. The girl was already wearing her tiara and she stood perfectly still as Lane pinned the flowing tulle skirt to the satin bodice. Kids were so easy to please, she thought. The kids were so different from the prima donna models she'd worked with at her fashion shows. Or the women she'd designed outfits for, who didn't think twice about having her tear the entire design apart and remake it because they suddenly wanted something better than so-and-so had last week. This little fairy princess was delighted with Lane's work.

She helped the girl take off the costume, easing it over her head.

"What do you think?"

"It's beautiful, Miss Douglas," Anna said, awed as a six-year-old could get. She raced off to tell her friends, and Lane noticed that the kids were getting wild and the mothers were looking plum worn-out. She did a quick measure of the children and their costume needs, then told Suzanne she could take care of the lot without the children being here to try them on. Suzanne was so grateful to be able to put her kids to bed, she promised a batch of homemade cookies for Lane's bookstore customers. Lane knew she could whip the costumes up in no time and saw no reason for mothers to chase children on sugar rushes this late at night.

Two hours later she heard, "Hey, I think you can stop now."

Just the sound of Tyler's voice set her blood humming. When she lifted her gaze, he was standing close, smelling like sawdust and aftershave, looking so rugged she nearly melted right out of the chair. She was in big trouble. She hadn't reacted to a man like this in…well, never.

Tyler caught the little flash in her eyes. "Man, when you agree to work, you work."

"I was in the zone," she said, trying to shrug off the nearly electrical zing popping through her blood.

Tyler's gaze moved over the costumes that were finished and hanging on a movable rack. He'd watched her off and on for the past two hours. She hadn't stopped for a moment, and she was fast, locked in a world of her own until he spoke to her.

"They're simple patterns," she said, brushing off his compliment.

"Sure, but you're nearly finished. And you did a great job."

"I still have trims and the fake buttons for the uniforms to do."

"There's always tomorrow."

"True," she said, leaning back in her chair with a tired sigh.

"Have dinner with me." She'd probably say no, he thought, but he had to give it a shot while her defenses were low.

She lifted her gaze to his. "We really are going to have trouble if you keep asking me the same question all the time, Tyler."

"Three times a charm…have dinner with me."

"No, thank you."

She looked as if she wanted to say yes, but for

whatever reason, she wasn't giving in. "You're a stubborn cuss," he said.

"And talking to you is impossible."

He grinned. "It's only dinner."

"Nothing is open at this hour." One thing she'd learned about this town was that, aside from a few select restaurants and a pizza joint, the streets rolled up at nine.

"Says who?" He stepped back and showed her the display of subs, chips and sodas on a table. The teenagers and other men were already chowing down in different areas of the stage.

She looked at him and smiled reluctantly. "Okay, I can't argue now."

Tyler hooked his thumbs in his jeans to keep from touching her and inclined his head to a spot on the far edge of the stage. She sat, her feet dangling over the edge, and he brought her a sandwich and a can of soda.

Then he hopped up beside her, his body shielding her from the rest of the volunteers.

"Those are the ugliest shoes I've ever seen on a woman," he said.

"You've made that point before." She looked down at the combat-boot-style shoe. "They're comfortable and warm. Like yours." She lightly kicked his foot. He wore something similar in dark tan. His had seen better days.

He simply stared at her for a minute. He didn't want to talk about shoes. He wanted to tell her how great she'd been. How much she'd impressed him with her talents and dedication. But all he could say was, "You amazed me. You just came in and took over."

She blinked wide eyes. "Oh, Lord, I did, didn't I? Do you think they'll be upset? It's their project and I'm the outsider."

Tyler smiled and shook his head. "It's the school's project, and did you see Suzanne dragging out of here? She was grateful for your help. They all were."

Lane shrugged. "It was fun, I admit it. How did you guys do?" she asked before he could question how she'd done so much work so fast.

Tyler cranked a look back over his shoulder at the stacks of plywood and sawhorses. And unfinished work. "We've got one more set to make and some painting to do, but that can wait till tomorrow."

"Tomorrow." She groaned.

"Service to the community," he reminded with a smile.

"I'm helping," she defended. "And the only reason I'm doing it is because your mother guilted me into this."

"I know. Do I know weaponry or what?"

She laughed softly.

"You have a great mouth, Lane. You should do that more often."

"I do laugh, at least twice a day."

"Just not around me."

"Fishing for compliments? I'd think with your fan club you wouldn't need more."

He frowned and Lane nodded toward a couple of young women who kept sliding glances at Tyler.

"They're children."

"They're in their twenties, McKay, and trying hard to get your attention."

He looked back at Lane. "Well, they're failing." But before she could make a wisecrack he said, "I know by your accent that you're not from around here, so what brought you to the South?"

Lane debated answering that and chose her words carefully. "Slow pace, beautiful scenery." Anonymity.

"Have you always sold books?"

"Yes." Another lie on top of the last one. But at this point, what did it matter? She was sitting at the tip of a mountain of lies and she kept having to scramble to keep from falling off.

"What made you take that old house and renovate it?"

No lies necessary here. "I fell in love with the place the instant I saw it, despite its hideous green paint. The house was like a genteel old woman. She was dying from neglect and cried out for a new dress and hairdo."

He smiled.

"What?" She snitched one of his chips.

"That's how I used to see the old homes around here. Not exactly like that, but like old souls that were fading. You know, my grandfather and father started out doing strictly renovations. McKay Construction didn't renovate yours, did we?"

"No, your competition did."

He clutched his heart, keeling over a little.

"Your company's bid was too high."

She'd removed the pickles from her sub and Tyler ate them. "Quality, my dear."

"Hey, they did a good job. And the renovation met the historical society's rules. And I did most of the restoration myself."

His brows shot up. "How'd you learn?"

She stared at him for a heartbeat, then said, "I read a book."

Behind them, at the back of the stage, people began cleaning up the mess, capping paint cans and collecting wood.

Yet Tyler kept his gaze on Lane, fascinated by the gold starburst in her deep-brown eyes. He wanted to see her without glasses, but it was like a prize he'd gain after a long journey. He could wait.

When she popped the last bite of her sub into her mouth, he reached out, a napkin curled in his fingers. She lurched back a little bit, but he kept coming, wiping the mustard off her jaw.

When his thumb rubbed across her lip, she gripped his wrist. "Tyler."

He twisted his hand around and caught hers. Heat pooled between them, sliding from her body in a pulse that rippled into him, then back again. His blood thickened, moving slower and hotter through his veins. For a heart-stopping moment, Tyler felt himself sinking. Her mouth was wide and plump, so damn kissable he wished they were alone. And that hungry thought surprised the hell out of him. He barely knew her. In fact, all he knew for sure was that she'd grabbed his curiosity and wouldn't let go.

A sharp bark of laughter from somewhere behind them dissolved the moment, and Tyler eased back, collecting their trash and standing on the stage.

He looked down at her, and then, as if even he

needed a break from whatever was burning between them, he shrugged and headed to the trash cans.

Lane looked down at the napkin in her hand, crushing it and battling with the schoolgirl-giddy feeling she always had when she was near Tyler. Okay, honest moment, she told herself. If you weren't hiding, if you hadn't had your heart smashed by Dan Jacobs and forced to keep secrets, would you want Tyler?

She looked slowly back over her shoulder. She'd be on him like a cat on a bowl of cream, she admitted silently. Her gaze traveled up his long, jean-clad legs to his wide shoulders. He might stay in an office all day and wear suits, but he sure as heck didn't look like it. He looked delicious.

He aimed a paper cup at the trash can and missed. Lane grinned as he bent to scoop the cup off the floor.

Behind him a girl was gathering wood planks and just as Tyler bent, the girl swung around to answer someone and smacked Tyler on the back of the head. He staggered.

"Tyler." Lane scrambled to her feet and shot across the stage as he folded to the ground.

The girl dropped the wood and apologized repeatedly as Lane slid to her knees beside Tyler.

He grabbed the back of his head, groaning. "Oh, man."

Lane probed the already swelling lump on the back of his head. No blood. "Just as I thought," she teased. "Your head's too hard to crack open."

"I'm wounded," he complained, turning his gaze on her. "Comfort me."

"Poor baby." She examined his eyes. She'd lost count of the number of times there were accidents at couture shows, and she was left to revive a starving model who'd fainted. His eyes were fine. Blue as the sky.

"Look at me, Tyler. What do you see?" She held up two fingers.

He grabbed them. "I see a sleeping beauty."

She rolled her eyes. "Stop flirting and answer me."

"I'm fine. Mmm…you smell good."

She looked up at the people gathered near. "Can you get me some ice? He's okay," she said to the girl who was in tears and clinging to her boyfriend.

Lane looked back at Tyler and felt a relief so profound it stunned her.

"I like you worrying over me," he said.

"I'd worry about anyone hit on the head," she said, though she admitted only to herself that her heart had skipped a few beats when she'd seen him slump over. "You're a danger to yourself. First my car, then this?"

Someone handed her ice wrapped in a rag and she put it to the back of his head. The rest of the crew went back to cleaning up.

A man asked if Tyler needed a lift home.

"I can drive," Tyler said, sitting up. "I've taken harder hits playing football."

"You're also not eighteen and full of invincibility," she said. "Besides, you've already proved you're not the best driver."

He shot her a look. "You're harping on that."

"Of course," she said smugly. "I'll drive you home."

He grinned.

"Oh, for heaven's sake." She stood and went for her purse, checked to see that her work area was cleaned up, then returned to him.

Tyler made a show of staggering and leaned on Lane.

"Oh, get off, you actor," she said, pushing him, but he clung to her, his arm heavy across her shoulder. Lane absorbed him, the warmth of his body, the scent of him. He toyed with a loose strand of hair and when she glanced his way, his lazy smile said his mind was leading elsewhere. She shook her head as if to shake him out of her system and pulled away when they reached her car.

Once inside, she started the engine, then pulled onto the street. It was deserted, a light evening rain coating the road with a glow that reflected the street lamps.

"Where do you live?"

He gave her directions and in minutes Lane pulled into the drive of the sprawling house. It was near the beach on the point, and she could hear the crash of waves. The wind was stronger and the scent of the sea surrounded her as she got out of the car.

Tyler moved up beside her and shook out the rag of ice chips on the lawn, where they sparkled like diamonds in the moonlight.

"Your home is beautiful," she said. "You live here alone?" The house had three floors—four if you counted the stilts that put the house twelve feet off the ground. That area was covered with ornate latticework to hide the garage beneath.

He smiled. "Glad you like it." They strolled up the walk.

"You built it, didn't you. All of it yourself." .

"Yeah. I started almost five years ago," Tyler said.

Without invitation, Lane moved up the Federal steps to the wide, wraparound porch. Although big enough to have tables and chairs, maybe a couple of swings, it was bare of furniture. The only decor was a forgotten fern drooping in the corner.

"It's gorgeous." The walkway and shrubbery was lit with tiny coach lanterns blending to a stone path leading off to the right and she assumed to the back of the house. What appeared to be a replica of an old carriage house was separated from the main house by a breezeway.

"That's your workshop, isn't it?" She pointed to the carriage house.

"Yes, it is."

"What to do make there?"

"I'm still doing some finishing work—mostly moldings. Want to see inside?"

Alarms went off. Inside in that big house alone with him? Her body was screaming, *Oh yes!* But her brain, thank heaven, was still in charge. "Another time, maybe."

"Come on in, Lane. Let me make some coffee."

She sighed, eyeing him. "Tyler, we both know what you want."

"I thought I was being subtle."

She laughed, short and sharp. "You? I'm not stupid. You just want to take me to bed."

He stepped closer, gazing down into her eyes. "I want to do more than *take* you to my bed, Lane."

Her insides clamped, blood rushing in her veins, making her skin tingle with heat. It had been a long time, too long since a man had looked at her with such open desire. The heat of it filled her, swamping her with needs she thought she'd managed to block out. "We've only just met. Don't be foolish."

Tyler didn't understand it, either. His body wanted this woman. His surge of testosterone was demanding he show her the fun they could have under the covers in long, slow kisses and hot sex. Desire was building to a height he'd never experienced before. He told himself it was the challenge she presented, that the harder she pushed, the harder he tried to get closer. He couldn't accept more than that and wouldn't. He was letting his body do some talking right now, but not his heart. That was staying out of the picture.

"I can't seem to help myself around you."

"At your age, you're blaming me for your raging hormones?" Lane said.

His brow furrowed and he saw something in her eyes he hadn't noticed before—shadows.

"Take some aspirin and go to bed," she said abruptly, needing to get as far away from Tyler as possible. "I'm not getting into a relationship with you or anyone. I know I'm just a challenge to you, so please back off."

The bite in her tone caught him off guard. "Lane, wait. That's not true."

She moved to the steps. "Good night, Tyler."

Before she could take the first one, he was there, grasping her upper arms and drawing her back. Her hand clutched his waist for balance, and for a moment, they just stared at each other.

"Don't."

"Maybe you started out as a challenge," he admitted. "But that's changed." His mouth was close, the warmth inviting her. "Come play with me."

She made a little sound, weak and almost panicked.

For a second she imagined herself going with him into his house, into his bed. Lying with him naked on cool sheets. Being desired and sharing more than words and a dinner out. The rush of need charging through her and clawing for that sweet moment of explosion. But it would be playing to him, nothing more. A game. Lane had been the tool of someone's game before.

The reality of her life hung over her like a looming dragon. Dan Jacobs, the tabloids, the suspicion of Mafia ties that cloaked her family. Because the news had hit the papers a week before her spring fashion show, it had bled over to her career and ruined her. In a few days she'd gone from being the hottest designer in Europe and New York to being the joke of the trade.

All of it kept her from having more than a casual friendship with Tyler, and even *that* was dangerous. She could lose too much and she liked her safe little world, wanted to keep it. That Tyler might learn the truth and bring attention to her was bad enough, but being with him longer than necessary, opening her heart to someone again, was just too big a risk.

"I can't."

"You can." He laid his mouth over hers.

Lane felt the floor vanish beneath her feet, the world of sound and sight folding up around her and sweeping her into a cocoon. With his strength, Tyler kept her prisoner, his mouth moving in slow lush waves over her. Patient. Trapping her soul. His tongue skimmed her lips, then pushed between them. Her fingers dug into his waist as the world tilted.

Mama mia, she'd forgotten that men could kiss like this.

Four

She was energy, pure kinetic energy, and with a kiss, she cooked him from the inside out. Slow and wet, the kiss turned rapidly stronger, pulling him into dark heat and evoking slick dreams of more. His imagination went crazy, thoughts of dragging her into his house, of stripping her down to her skin and making love to her in the foyer pelted him like hard rain. He wanted her right this second, and need rippled up his body in a hot charge. But he wasn't so caught up that he didn't realize one thing.

She didn't deny herself, but she didn't surrender completely, either.

He felt it; that she wouldn't sink into him, that she wouldn't touch him more than her mouth on his and her hand at his waist. She held herself back, and the thought of what it would be like if she didn't made him groan. He started to close his arms around her, push his hand into her hair. But she stepped back abruptly. Tyler felt as if his limbs went with her and experienced overwhelming disappointment.

She blinked and stared. Heat poured off her in waves with her labored breath, and by the look on her face, she was just as stunned as he was.

"No, Tyler."

"That felt like a yes to me, darlin'." He reached for her. "Come back here."

Her gaze searched his, quickly, briefly. "I can't do this, not with you," she said in a strained voice, then turned and hurried down the steps, then damn near ran. He'd never had a woman head for the hills like that, and he frowned at her back. Her hair had come undone, tumbling over her shoulders as she climbed into her car. Seconds later she was pulling out of the driveway. She never looked up, never looked back. He knew because he watched her.

Tyler sagged against the porch post, raking his hand through his hair. He winced at the sore spot on the back of his skull. The pain was running a close second to the ache in the rest of him.

The rain started up again, and Tyler fished in his pocket for his house keys and went inside. He stood in the foyer, the house echoing with emptiness. And he felt as if he'd just let something wonderful slip away.

Lane braked at the stoplight and dropped her head onto the cool steering wheel. *Get a grip*. She swallowed once, twice, but it wasn't much help. Her insides were stinging with sensations, and her heart was pounding like a jackhammer, making her body hotter than it already was. And it was boiling. Leaning back, she blew out a breath and pulled at her scarf, then opened her jacket, fanning the lapels. Then she opened the car window to let in the cool night air. To no avail.

Her mouth was tender and swollen from his kiss. And from that one kiss, she knew she was in trouble. Tyler was imprinted on her.

It had been the look in his eyes that really struck home. He wanted her, and he didn't seem to care that she'd intentionally made herself look unattractive. That she hid behind a bun and big glasses and wore no makeup and mud-colored oversize clothes.

Yup, she was in real trouble. The disguise wasn't working on him. She wondered when he'd see through it completely and understand that she'd lied about everything.

That couldn't happen. She couldn't *let* that happen.

She didn't want Tyler to hate her and she had a sneaking suspicion that hiding her identity and her appearance wasn't going to go over very well with him. But there were other things to consider.

Like Dan Jacobs. At any moment he could come rushing back into her life and open up the chest of secrets and humiliation she'd left behind when she'd changed her name and walked away from her career and family. Dan Jacobs had been paid for a story, for the exposé on her family's supposed Mafia connections. She'd intercepted a phone call at her own apartment that revealed exactly who and what he was. And why he'd seduced her. It wouldn't matter to anyone that the account books of Giovanni Wineries hadn't even hinted at money laundering. Her father had given the winery books to the FBI, she had given the agency hers, too. It had been hearsay, rumor, and it had ruined her. There was nothing to connect her family to the Mafia except a few paparazzi photos of her brother with questionable businessmen. Why her brother Angel was with those men was still a mystery to her, but regardless, Dan Jacobs would plaster lies across the papers and bring it all up again. He was that much of a snake. She'd lose her privacy. She wanted to yell at Angel for getting involved, however slightly, with the mob and not caring what it did to the rest of the family.

In her heart she believed Angel was innocent, but she couldn't let that mess touch Tyler, either. He was a nice guy. Stubborn, hardheaded, but oh man, he oozed sex appeal. And she was falling for him.

Damn him for kissing her, she thought, stepping on the gas and heading toward home. It made her feel more alone than ever. Because if she wanted a real life, a private life without news crews, Dan Jacobs and his exposé, she couldn't have anything more to do with a man who was newsworthy enough to bring attention right to her door.

As much as Tyler McKay was a danger to her privacy, all she wanted was to open the door and let him in. And that scared her the most.

Tyler threw down his pen and, bracing his elbows on his desk, gripped his head. After two days, the lump on the back of his skull was gone, but the soreness reminded him of Lane—and kissing her. Heck, he didn't need a crack on the head to remember what her mouth felt like on his. Lush, full…earthy. Just thinking about it made his muscles tighten and his blood simmer. He groaned and leaned back in the leather chair, swinging it toward the window. Beyond the glass, he had the most spectacular view of the low country, but it didn't keep his thoughts off Lane.

He wanted to see her.

And he *didn't* want to see her.

She was more than a puzzle, and that made her dangerous to the freedom he coveted. His interest alone was gaining speed. He knew that under all those ugly clothes and even uglier shoes was a tigress locked in a cage. The single kiss had told him that. And the temptation to see if he had the key was killing him.

But she wouldn't let him near again. She'd kept him at arm's length since their first meeting, made it clear that she'd wanted to be left alone. It was *why* she wanted to be left alone that intrigued him. He'd never met a woman who tried so hard not to be noticed.

Unlike his ex-fiancée, Clarice, who had wanted the world to see her and made a show of her entrance into a room just to get attention. Over the past two years, Tyler had asked himself what had made him propose marriage to Clarice. She'd had beauty and grace and had come from a good background, and he'd thought he truly loved her. But she'd lied about her love for him, and that was the deepest cut of all. After her betrayal, it hadn't taken long for the love to die, but the pain lingered. The humiliation of can-

celing the society wedding of the decade, stuck with
him. All their plans had been part of her web of lies.
A disguise to get what she wanted—his family name,
family money. The one thing he couldn't tolerate was
lying.

He shook off the memories, and then thoughts of
Lane instantly popped into his mind. She didn't care
about his name or his money. She didn't even want
him around long enough to get her car repaired.

That was Lane's allure. When a woman played
hard to get, a man played harder to get her. He
grinned at the thought. And if you get her, then what?
He asked himself. Love her and leave her gracefully?
What did that say about him? That he only wanted
surface feelings from a woman? A little sex and
cocktails?

He stared at his reflection in the window glass,
disgusted with himself. Lane had more beneath the
surface than he expected, and he'd sat at work for
two days fighting the urge to go see her. Lane had a
lock on him that Clarice had never had. Instinct told
him to leave her alone. Hell, instinct told him to run
like mad in the other direction. To let her go and
keep that kiss as nothing more than a memory.

It would be wiser if he wanted to keep his heart
out of play. He could do it. He could see her and
date her. Wherever this was going, he wasn't looking
for Mrs. Tyler McKay.

Man, when did you get so arrogant? The woman
can barely stand being near you, and you're wondering if she has sights on marriage? And who's to
say that it would lead to anything like that? Especially if she didn't want it to lead anywhere at all.

Even as a voice inside him said, *Be afraid, be very afraid,* Tyler swirled the chair around and tapped the intercom on his phone. "Martha, I'm going out to lunch."

"Yes, sir." A pause and then, "Really, sir?"

He smiled. "Yes, really." He understood her surprise. Lately he rarely left the office for anything but meetings.

"Shall I make a reservation for you?"

"No, thank you, but what's that restaurant, the one you and my mother rave about? The broken something?"

"Oh, that would be the Cracked Crab," his secretary said quickly. "I have a menu if you want me to call your order in so it's ready for you."

"Excellent," he said, glancing at his watch. Since Lane liked to keep her guard up, a little surprise was in order to bring it down.

Lane looked up as the bell over the door tinkled and Tyler strolled into her shop. Everything inside her went on alert. Dressed in a thousand-dollar navy suit, he looked good enough to eat. And damn, when he was near, she was hungry.

"We're closed for the next hour," she said.

"I know."

He reached the counter and stopped, staring at her. Lane felt heat race up from her throat.

"Why are you here?" she asked.

"Taking you to lunch."

"You should have called. I have plans."

He frowned. "With who?"

Her cat and paperwork, she thought. "I don't think that's any of your business, Tyler."

"After that kiss, I'm making it mine."

"Oh, really," she said through clenched teeth. "Well, you're wrong. A kiss does not mean I'm your business, and I don't have time for lunch. I close the shop because I use the time to catch up on paperwork." She gathered and racked papers to prove her point.

"Or hide," he said.

She looked up.

"Or run."

"I didn't run."

"Woman, you took off faster than a cat after a mouse, and you know it."

"I simply left."

"At marathon speed." He leaned over the counter. "You're afraid of me."

"No, I'm afraid of me."

He frowned deeply.

"I don't want to be something to you, because you have a certain reputation...."

His brows shot up. "Hey, I'm a nice guy. Ask anyone."

He looked adorably defensive. Darn it. "I don't have to ask. I've heard. You don't stay with a woman for longer than a month or two and, frankly, after that kiss, I'm not ready to be another notch on your belt."

There, she'd found an easy excuse, a way to get rid of him. It was sensible, though she didn't really believe the rumors she'd heard about him being a playboy. A man who enjoyed playing didn't have to be untrustworthy or amoral. And the way he'd spoken to his mother said a lot about him.

But as she'd planned for the past two days, it was a way to put him off—when she really wanted to see what it was like to wear him like a second skin. The thought made her blood sizzle and she looked down at the papers in front of her.

"So I have a bad reputation?"

She smiled to herself. "The worst." What a lie.

"Well, then, date me and change it."

"No."

"Lunch?"

"I have work to do."

"I went to the Cracked Crab for it."

Her head jerked up as he set the small basket on the counter. It was her favorite restaurant, and she'd become good friends with the owner, Nalla Campanelli, a woman of Italian and Irish descent, like her. They'd hit it off from day one, and Lane got to be the taste tester for Nalla's latest creations.

She eyed the basket. "What's in it?"

Tyler felt victory looming and hid a smile. "Thai crab salad. Nalla said it was your favorite."

Lane hesitated. It was indeed her favorite. "With the little cracked-pepper crackers?"

Tyler grinned. "I think so. Look, if we're not going to eat this, then I'll take it back to the office." He started to move away.

She reached. "No!" She met his gaze. "You are so sneaky."

"I know."

That smile blinded her again. She inclined her head and they went over to the cappuccino bar. She took the basket, her mouth already watering as Tyler pulled a table and two chairs close.

Lane nabbed some plates from behind the coffee bar, then ignored the chairs and knelt on the rug, pulling back the cloth, decorated with little red crabs, that covered the basket. "Nalla is the best."

"So I heard. Martha thinks so, too."

"Martha?" Lane asked, frowning and ignoring the little prick of jealousy she felt.

"My secretary."

"They call them executive assistants now, you know."

"Not her. She's a holdover from when my dad ran the company. She's sixty-three, her dependable shoes squeak, and she still takes shorthand."

"I bet she's efficient as heck, too." Lane opened the containers and spooned the meal onto plates.

"She practically runs my life." Tyler took off his jacket and sat in a chair, watching her.

Lane could feel it. His eyes had fingers, and she could feel them probing her face, bringing back the memory of his soul-stripping kiss. Her hands shook a little at the thought of kissing him, of feeling him pressed against her in full body contact.

Don't.

Don't go there. It will bring too much attention. *He* will bring attention and then he'll find out the truth about you and hate you for lying. She chanted the warning silently so she wouldn't forget. So she wouldn't melt when he looked at her. She handed him a plate of Thai crab, then started savoring each bite of her own.

"Where do you live?" he asked.

With a fork, she poked the air over her head to indicate that she lived above the shop.

"It can't be that big."

She chewed and swallowed. "It's not. I don't need much room."

"I know what you mean. I rattle around my house like a stray dog looking for a place to settle."

She stilled, her fork halfway to her mouth. Her look said, *Explain.*

He set the plate on the little table. "It's almost as if I don't live there, as if I just visit every night."

"Not a home yet, then."

He shrugged. "It has all my stuff in it."

"Maybe you need to hire a decorator to get the feeling you want."

Lane wasn't going to mention that *things* did not make a home. That would lead to discussions about what did, and getting into a conversation about love and family with Tyler McKay was not wise. She knew without asking that despite the wealth and privilege they'd both had growing up, his ideas about family hadn't been anything like the one she'd grown up around.

"The idea of dealing with a decorator gives me chills." Suddenly he slid to the floor before her, the motion bringing him closer.

She gave him a wary look and scooted back. "Ask your mother for help."

"Hey, I want it to look like *my* house, not the one I grew up in."

"Good point." Lane had grown up in a penthouse in New York and a villa in Tuscany. Her great-grandparents' home in Rapolano Terme, Tuscany, where the winery had begun and where the company headquarters was now. And when her career had exploded during her fashion show, she'd left only a suite of rooms in a hotel in Paris behind. It was tough to stick around when no one was buying her fashion designs and the press was pasting headlines like *Giovanni Designs Sewn with Mafioso Thread,* and *Giovanni Sales High—an Offer You Can't Refuse,* instead of fashion reports. Inwardly she groaned at the memory and ate more crab. Though a need for a vat of chocolate was creeping up on her.

"Why books?" Tyler asked, wondering about that sad look she got sometimes.

"Why construction?"

"Uh-uh." He wagged a finger at her. "Mine's a family business."

"Did you want to take it over?"

He shrugged. "It's all I've known. My dad dragged me and my brothers along to the construction sites when we were old enough to know the rules and not get into trouble. I was fascinated that from stacks of lumber and nails a home grew, then a business."

"Then a conglomerate, a regional corporation," she added.

A little alarm went off inside him, and he stared at the top of her head as she bent over the basket. "Checking me out?"

"I read the papers, McKay." She pulled out the little package of crackers. "I love these." She opened it and handed him one. He nibbled, watching her as she put a dollop of Thai crab on the cracker and devoured it.

"You really like this, huh?"

"Don't you?"

He shrugged. He hadn't even tasted it yet, since he was too busy watching her. She sat cross-legged on the floor, her navy skirt covering her legs and ugly shoes. He liked that she didn't nibble and worry about fat content and calories like most women he'd been with. No, he thought, don't compare her to other women. She's definitely different.

"What I like best is Nalla's creations. They change a little with her mood."

He scoffed. "What in this world doesn't change with a woman's mood?"

She looked up, eyes wide as she swallowed. She thought about that. "Football?"

He grinned and tried the food. It was delicious.

"I love to eat, especially when someone else makes it," Lane said.

"Do you cook?"

She tasted the marinated cucumbers and tomato salad that Nalla had created only last week. "Taking inventory or something?"

He smiled. "Are you ever going to give me a straight answer?"

"Not if I can help it. Adds to the mystery."

"You have enough going on, Lane, trust me."

"Then I'll spare you my Mata Hari routine. Men can't resist me then. Can't you tell?" She gestured to the empty store.

"I get first dibs."

Her smile was genuine, and Tyler felt his entire body tighten. "So?" he asked.

"So what?

"Do you cook?"

"Yes, I can cook, but rarely do it. It's not much fun when it's just for me."

"Any good at it?"

She was half Italian. Cooking was in her genes. "Decently enough." Her brows drew down a fraction. "You're fishing for a dinner invitation?"

"Why not? You're having lunch with me now."

"The Thai crab made the decision and you asked. I didn't."

He blinked. "I think I'm insulted."

"Don't be. But I told you, Tyler, I don't want a relationship or anything from you. You're the most eligible, well-known bachelor in this city. And you're just chasing me because I'm immune to the McKay charm."

Was that the only reason? he wondered, then remembered kissing her. "You weren't immune the other night on my porch."

"Pity kiss," she said, and snickered a little. What a lie. She'd almost begged him for more.

He laughed, the sound deep and rough, then took the cracker she was about to eat. "If that was pity, then I want to try one on for size when you really want to kiss me."

So did she. Boy, did she.

He ate the cracker in one bite, then leaned closer, tipping his head, and she understood his intention instantly.

She inched back. "You have crab breath."

"So do you."

She put her fingers over his mouth. "Stop this. Please."

He kept his features schooled, but she was serious. Even her eyes turned sad. He realized his past had indeed caught up with him and was ruining what could be a very good thing.

She lowered her hand. "Just be my friend."

He made a sour face. "Okay, that's a definite passion killer." Tyler went back to eating, and though he didn't want to believe that his supposed playboy reputation was the real heart of her excuse, he'd accept it for now. Changing the subject entirely, he asked, "Where were you last night? We were all working on the pageant."

"My part was done."

He looked at her, frowning.

"I finished it all the next evening. All the costumes are in the dressing room tagged with the actors' names."

"So what you're saying is, community service is over."

Lane felt suddenly, strangely alone as she said, "Yes. It is."

She watched as Tyler leaned closer, his hand on the floor near her hip, hemming her in. He met her gaze. "If you think I'm going to go away now, Lane, you're wrong. Dead wrong."

Lane experienced true panic—and complete and utter joy.

Five

Tyler was what Lane's Nana would call a *noodge*. He'd turned up in the past couple of days in the oddest places. Like the drugstore as she was walking out the door. Or over at Nalla's place while Lane was getting the chance to taste the chef's newest version of shrimp-and-crab fettuccini. Though she'd like to think the reason behind his sudden appearance was just to see her, she knew it was to get her to join the festival. But this time he'd found her in the grocery store between the guavas and the bananas.

And this time, he'd brought backup—the head of the business association, his brother, Kyle.

Big surprise there.

"I'm feeling a little persecuted here, fellas," she said, her gaze shifting between the two men. They both flushed with embarrassment, and Lane recognized the undercurrent of accusation between siblings. She could almost imagine the you-started-it-no-you-did battle when they were younger.

"Lane, your shop is near the main avenue and you're the only one not participating in the Winter Festival. It's not required of members of the business association, but not taking part will make you stand out more than you realize."

"Uncle," she said.

"Uncle who?" Tyler said.

Lane sent him a patient look. He understood perfectly well. "I said 'Uncle', I give in, you have a victory. I'll join the festival completely." Lane knew when to concede defeat. She'd had to do it more than once in the past two years, and she understood only too well when she couldn't fight the fight to win the war. Not that she was at war with Tyler. She didn't know *what* she was with Tyler. But she figured that if she stopped trying so hard to get him out of her life, he might accept victory and go lavish his attention on someone new.

Instantly a stab of something close to pain shot through her chest, and images of his arms around another woman stung. Yet another warning that she was already falling for the man—as if she needed another warning. That kiss and how deeply it penetrated her guard was plenty.

Just being near the man made her blood sing.

"Excellent," Kyle said, handing her a packet. He was a nearly identical version of his older brother, tall, muscled, with that charismatic McKay smile. Deadly.

Lane looked at the packet, then at him.

"It's the rules and requirements," Kyle explained. "The festival is a big tourist draw. The council made some restrictions, mostly with alcohol."

She nodded. She sold books, coffee and Nalla's muffins, so alcohol restrictions weren't a problem.

"I'm glad you're participating, Lane," Kyle said softly, his smile slow and sexy. Good grief, she thought. A girl didn't stand a chance around these two.

"To be honest, Nalla Campanelli convinced me before today."

At that, Kyle's gaze narrowed and darkened. Tyler cleared his throat softly. And Lane wondered what was going on between her friend and this man. Interesting. Whatever it was, it wasn't good. And it was old news. Nalla hadn't mentioned anything about Kyle McKay before, and Lane never pried because she didn't want anyone prying into her past. But Nalla was the only person in this town who knew her real identity. It was almost good that Nalla wasn't fond of a McKay.

"I still don't see how a bookshop could make a difference in a street festival."

"Your lattes and cappuccinos could, and if the chilly weather holds up, you'll do great."

Chilly? December in the South was not considered cold by Northerners. Not even brisk. It was one thing she loved about South Carolina, yet a little voice reminded her how hot it had been only three months ago. She'd hadn't chosen Bradford for its weather, but for the old-fashioned charm and slow pace, and because it was off the beaten path of anything reporter Dan Jacobs might stumble on. Everything had been great. Quiet. Until she'd met Tyler.

She looked up from the papers, meeting his gaze, and he looked a little concerned by her silence.

"I was just thinking that I'll have to hire help," she said quickly. "I can't run the store and participate in the street festival from a vendor's wagon at the same time."

Tyler was quick to say, "Diana Ashbury's youngest daughter is home from college, and she needs a temporary job."

Lane eyed Tyler. "Well, it seems you've thought of everything, haven't you?"

"I try." He wasn't the least bit ashamed about maneuvering her into this.

Flashing his brother a strange look, Kyle said goodbye and strolled out of the grocery store, leaving Tyler and Lane staring at each other in the produce aisle. "Why are you pushing this so much?" she asked him quietly.

"Good for business."

True but very lame, she thought. Moving away, Lane bagged some fruit and vegetables, then pushed the cart farther down the aisle. Tyler was right beside her, smiling at people he knew, which was almost everyone. She could already see the gossip brewing on the air.

"It's the middle of the week—do you even work for a living?"

"I'm the boss, so I get to make the rules."

She rolled her eyes. Who could resist that grin? "Why would you care about my business?"

"I care about you."

She stopped and met his gaze again. "You don't even know me, Tyler."

"I'm trying to rectify that, but you're not cooperating."

"You're not getting the message."

"I'm naturally hardheaded."

She laughed softly, and selected items quickly. She needed to be out of here and away from Tyler, or at least out of the public eye.

"You're really going to eat that?"

She looked down at the tin of anchovies and, shaking her head, put it back on the shelf.

He inched closer, his voice low. "I'm making you nervous."

"No, yes. No," she finally decided, annoyed with him. "Just really confused."

His smile fell. "How so?"

She tipped her head. "I don't know what your angle is. You keep showing up and working your way into my life, and I'm wondering if it's real interest or if I'm just another gotta-have-it-because-I-can't conquest."

"I thought you'd at least know me better than that by now."

"I don't know you at all." Except that he was handsome, stubborn and a great kisser. Her body responded to the memory of their kiss, and she hurriedly selecting items off the shelf. If she didn't get out of here she'd probably attack him in the middle of the grocery store.

"We're back to me trying to change that."

She looked at him. "For pity's sake, talking to you is like talking to wood."

"Give me one reason you don't want to see me."

Because I want you, she thought and quickly buried that idea. "I'm just not interested in a relationship, and like I mentioned before, you have a lousy reputation."

"That's weak."

"Oh, really? Look around us and tell me we aren't being watched—intently."

He did and they were. "It's a small town."

"My point exactly. You might have the name and stamina to weather gossip and whatever comes along, but I don't."

He reared back. "You won't see me *because* I'm a McKay." No doubt a first for him, she thought.

When she didn't respond, Tyler's gaze narrowed on her. "My family is not me, Lane. But they come with the package. I can't help who I am."

"Neither can I."

He leaned nearer, his hand closing over hers on the cart handle. His eyes were intense and simmering with something she'd never seen before. The calm and charm were gone, and all that was left was pure Tyler.

"I don't know who hurt you so badly that you're terrified of being with me," he growled lowly. "But I'd like to punch the jerk."

Her eyes rounded. Then he kissed her. Nothing sweet and soft for the public, but a deep kiss of lips and tongue that curled her toes and left her electrified and breathless. Customers gasped and giggled, though she barely heard them over the roaring in her ears. All she saw was Tyler, inches from her and filling her with heated emotion she wasn't sure she was ready to accept.

"Just so you know, darlin', I don't intend to keep taking the blame for him," Tyler said.

He made an about-face and walked away, leaving her alone between the pork chops and chicken.

And like every time he was near, she didn't know whether to be happy or scared.

Tyler climbed into his car and slammed the door, his angry gaze on the store. Someone had done a number on Lane. He should just walk away. He didn't want to work past the damage left by another man. But he'd already tried staying away from her and hadn't lasted forty-eight hours. He was trying his best to take it slowly, to charm his way into her good graces. And he was failing miserably. He started the engine of the rental car, wanting his own Jaguar back, then shifted gears, and pulled out of the parking lot. He'd get her car fixed and that would be it. She'd have to come to him.

He'd driven half a block before he wondered why he was making demands on a woman who'd love for him to get lost. If he truly believed that, he reasoned, he would disappear. But he didn't believe it. Lane Douglas had something special, and he admitted he was enjoying breaking down her barriers, one by one. Soon, she'd tell him what had happened to make her erect so many walls. Tyler just wanted to scale them one at a time. Because their kisses spoke of more than just desire. Hell, it practically screamed power and fire, something he hadn't had in a very long time. He was surprised that he wanted to discover more.

He'd put strict rules on his relationships since Clarice had betrayed him, and he was man enough to admit that while they sounded good in practice, they made him feel a little superficial. Why should he expect more from a woman than he was giving himself?

Charming his way into Lane's life was more work than he'd ever had to do with a woman, and she still kept everything from him. Everything. Yet like a glutton for punishment, he kept coming back. That alone was a message he couldn't ignore, and if he was honest with himself, he was tired of being cautious.

The pageant launched the Winter Festival. Lane attended the children's play, smiling at the little toy soldiers and fairies, thinking she'd never seen anything so adorable in her life. The children looked as if they were having as much fun as the audience. Missed lines produced giggles, and one girl kept nudging a toy soldier until the boy nearly fell over. Lane had gone to private schools, and as a kid she'd never been involved in anything like this. But the sight of the kindergartners, so small and filled with wonder, opened up a longing she didn't think she had. While the choir sang, she wondered if she'd ever have children of her own, wondered if she'd be a good mother.

And who would she love enough to want to make those babies with? Tyler's face blossomed in her mind and she immediately cut the fantasy short. There was really no point in dreaming, she thought sadly. He'd never forgive her if he knew the truth, and to tell him the truth she'd have to trust him.

She didn't trust anyone. Except maybe Nalla. Yet while the children performed in the costumes she'd made, she felt more involved with the townspeople than she had in a year and a half. She liked people. She missed being with people. She missed a lot of things she'd thought she wouldn't.

Her career had surrounded her with fashion buyers, designers, models, reporters, photographers and textile merchants. Her own family was large and loud. Sure, they'd been in the papers a lot, the rich and notorious always were, but holidays were just like anyone else's—huge dinners, gift exchanging and traditions. When they were all together. In the past eight years, those moments had been rare. Her parents lived separately, which wasn't a bad thing, though they were still legally married. Just too different to live in the same house. Lane accepted the fact that her mother was a little shallow and that she liked nightlife, traveling and being seen a smidgen more than she liked motherhood. Her father tended his vineyards as though they were another crop of children. As if she and her five siblings weren't enough. Lane forgot about the people around her, the children singing, and was still thinking about her father and missing him when the play ended.

See your good fortune, Elaina, her Papa would say. *Why would you want more?* There was more. She'd known it when she'd been with Dan—even if it was one-sided, a complete lie and had lasted less than a year. She'd loved Dan, and sunk her whole heart into their relationship and had become lovers. For a while, it was wonderful, till he betrayed her. Yet there was a certain dark-haired man with a killer smile she blamed for making her even think of wanting more.

As the crowd filed out of the town theater, Lane received dozens of compliments on the costumes from proud parents, and she felt their warmth and good wishes flow through her like warm honey. Soon she was standing on the street in front of the old theater. Her gaze moved over the historical section of town. Bay Street ran through the center, near the river, then curved sharply to the area where her shop was located. While her end of the street hadn't been decorated yet, and she supposed some of that was up to her, on Bay the banners for the street dance were already up and flapping in the cool evening air. The construction of the stage near the waterfront park was nearly completed. Someone had strung lights on it already, and they twinkled like a ship in the harbor. She'd be able to hear the music from her shop.

Her vendor's cart would be at the waterfront, and her store would be open later. She hoped Peggy Ashbury, Diana's nineteen-year-old daughter, could handle the crowd. In the store she was doing fine already, and Lane was glad she'd hired her. Diana liked the ten-percent employee discount, too. Lane headed toward home.

After a few steps she heard, "Hi."

She jerked around. "Tyler. I didn't see you in there."

"I was backstage moving sets."

A millionaire moving children's stage sets. It made her smile. Tyler was so different from the men she'd dated before coming to Bradford. Money and privilege hadn't affected him, which was an attraction all on its own, she decided. He was involved in everything, wasn't above lending a hand, getting dirty. And right now he had paint smears on his hands.

"Not quite dry?" She pointed to them.

"Cheap paint." He rubbed at it. "I know this is going to sound really high schoolish, but can I walk you home?"

She smiled, shoving her hands deep into her pockets. "Sure."

He fell into step beside her, and they strolled without speaking for a few moments. Then he said, "I saw you running the other night on the beach."

She glanced his way. "A girl has to stay in shape."

"Who would know under all those clothes?"

"I beg your pardon?"

He loved that indignant look of hers. "I saw you in leggings and a sweatshirt, Lane." He whistled softly.

"Oh, for heaven's sake, it was too dark to see anything." Exactly the reason she ran at night.

He knew that, but he liked teasing her. "I'm a man—I have chick radar." He paused and then said, "And binoculars."

Lane laughed deeply and Tyler wanted to hear more. The breeze offered a whiff of her perfume, spicy, a little citrusy. It didn't fit the picture he was seeing. Her hair pulled back in a tight bun and the round glasses, slipped low on her nose so often she had to keep pushing them up. Dowdy. Bookish. Then he remembered the woman running like a deer on the beach at midnight.

"You're not what you appear to be."

Everything inside her went on full alert. "How so?"

He leaned closer. "Kiss one and kiss two for starters."

"You're counting?"

"I'm hoping for a matched set. Six or eight, to start."

She laughed again, and when he took her hand, she didn't pull back. "You're impossible."

"Impossibly handsome? Mom thinks so."

"Impossibly stubborn and persistent. Also a dreamer."

"Since you didn't add arrogant, ugly and a pest, I consider myself on your good side." Tyler squeezed her hand and continued walking. "Being a dreamer's not a bad thing. Don't you have dreams?"

She shrugged. "Sure." For a real life, she thought suddenly, and wondered where that had come from. "But I have what I want." So why was seclusion getting to her all of a sudden? She refused to attribute her dissatisfaction to him. She got this way every few months and would deal with it as she always had— ignore it. But since the temptation to come out of hiding was overwhelming, it often made her angry.

"Is keeping this wall around yourself part of what you want?"

She shot him a look and tried to shake off his hand. He wouldn't let her go and stopped in the middle of the sidewalk. Overhead, the Spanish moss hanging from tree limbs swayed in the breeze. Cars drove past, ignoring the couple under the glow of an antique streetlamp.

His gaze raked her features. "Who hurt you, Lane?"

She looked away. What was she going to say now? "It's not important."

He put a finger under her chin, forcing her to look at him. "It is to me."

She knew Tyler well enough to know he wasn't going to give up easily, and she already felt backed into a corner. "Okay, fine, since I know you'll badger me for the next block. The man I was seeing betrayed me." *Used me, said he loved me, then the night after I learned that Richard Damon, photographer, was really Dan Jacobs, freelance reporter, he took our entire relationship, everything I'd said to him in confidence about my family, my dreams, and exposed my most intimate feelings in the newspapers for the world to read. With pictures.*

"How?"

"The details aren't important. I loved and trusted him and he betrayed my feelings in the worst way." And what difference was there in what she was doing to Tyler by keeping secrets? She had good reasons, really good ones. If her life was exposed, he'd get hurt in the process, just as she had from her brother Angel's troubles. Besides, she'd loved Dan. She didn't love Tyler and he didn't have those feelings for her, so what did it matter right now? Why couldn't he just let it be?

Tyler could see Lane's temper rising, her eyes practically sparkling with anger. She didn't like remembering her pain any more than he did, and he felt like a creep for prying. Tyler tried not to push, but this jerk had hurt her enough that she kept everyone out. He suspected that Nalla Campanelli was her only friend. It saddened him.

"He was a moron," Tyler said.

She looked up. "Maybe I was the real fool, Tyler, for trusting him."

"Don't blame yourself. The ability to trust is a blessing. Anyone who betrays that trust doesn't deserve to be in your life. Look at it that way."

"Sometimes I think he'd intended to betray me all along." She sighed. "Which of course, makes me an idiot for not seeing it from the start." She released a sigh, and with it went some tension. But she didn't say anything more.

They continued walking; she leaned into him a bit, didn't try to withdraw her hand from his. He hadn't asked her to elaborate, but he wished he could climb into her mind. At least he had an idea now of why she was so reserved with people. Mostly with him. Getting badly burned taught you ways to avoid getting singed again. He ought to know.

Wasn't that the reason he'd had only casual relationships since his engagement ended? To keep a distance so that no one would get close enough to hurt him again? A man didn't have to be kicked in the teeth twice.

Tyler bent his arm, the motion bringing her closer to his side, and he felt like a teenager with his first girl. It was weird. He was thirty-four, for crying out loud. Yet his heart was thumping like a bass drum, and all he wanted to do was back her into a corner and kiss her. He was even thinking like a teenager, all hormones and fantasies.

"This is me," she said, pointing to the shop.

He looked up at the second floor. "Aren't you going to invite me up to your place for coffee or a nightcap?"

She pushed her glasses up her nose. "I don't drink, and coffee this late will keep me awake."

"Yes or no would've done fine, Lane. You don't have to make excuses."

She threw her hands up and let them fall. "*Now* you tell me. And here I thought 'Go away' was clear."

She noticed that his brow knit, though his smile remained. "Are you trying to be cute?"

"Ducks and bunnies are cute, McKay."

"You're no bunny." He inched closer—and she let him. Little alarms were pinging inside her, but Lane ignored them as she stared into his eyes. A girl could get lost in those blue depths and like it, she thought.

"You walked me home for a kiss, didn't you?"

He tugged at the collar of her jacket. "Yup."

"I should have set you straight then."

"Set me straight now, Lane. I'm feeling crooked and dastardly." He gave his best villain laugh.

She grinned. "You're something else, McKay." She brushed back a strand of hair that had fallen over his forehead, then rose on her toes and kissed him. Just as quickly she hopped back, shocked at herself. "Oh, damn. I didn't mean to… I shouldn't have—"

He latched on to her jacket lapels and pulled her against him. "Shoulda, coulda, woulda," he muttered, saying the last against her mouth. His tongue swept over her lips, then slid deep inside. He devoured her mouth. There was no other word for it.

He kissed her as if he was dying, as if he'd never have another chance. Taste, nibble, plunge, taste some more. Each touch gathered her desire like a tether and pulled her along at a dizzying speed. Her head was spinning, her blood rushing, and she sank into the dark, hot pleasure of his mouth.

He molded her body to his length. Full contact. She could feel his rock-hard arousal.

It was divine. His strong arms closed more tightly, and while he was going to know she wasn't all layers of ugly clothes, she didn't care. Not at this moment. All she wanted was a little bit more, to keep her company in her lonely nights. But when his hand moved down her spine and pressed her hips to his, Lane's head went light. How could it not, with all her blood rushing through her body and looking for a place to settle? Then it did. In the center of her, the very core that was a jumble of pumping sensations and blood and pure liquid desire. She pushed her fingers into his hair and held on as his lips and tongue played over hers with exquisite skill. Oh, yes. She wanted to feel him—touch his chest, touch something more than his hair and preferably while naked, and just when she thought she'd drag him upstairs for more than a nightcap, he stopped and let her go.

Lane staggered, grabbing the wrought-iron fence to keep from melting into a puddle at his feet.

"There are some things I don't want anyone in this town to see," Tyler said, shoving his hands in his jean pockets and struggling for his next breath. His groin was thick and aching, and every muscle in his body was so tight and taut he thought if he moved

too fast, he'd snap in two. He looked at Lane through
hooded eyes. All hot and flustered, she was sexier
than ever before.

He wanted her in his bed, naked, hair down,
glasses gone, and open for him. He really should stop
thinking like that in public. Especially when his body
shouted reaction like a beacon.

"See you tomorrow, Lane."

"Tomorrow?" she croaked. Just where had her
breath gone now? Why wouldn't her lungs fill?

"Yes, I'm volunteer crowd control." He backstepped down the street, one hand shoved deep into
his jacket pocket while the other twirled the ends of
an imaginary mustache. "And guess where my post
is?" He waggled his brows.

Lane's gaze moved to the small poster tacked to
the lamppost and marking the spot in front of her
shop, then to Tyler. He was already fading into the
darkness, that villain laugh floating back to her on
the night breeze.

Oh, dear. What mixed signals had she just given
him?

But Lane knew they weren't mixed, but right on
target with his.

Six

___

The streets practically vibrated with the bass from the band on the waterfront. Oldies and country-western music followed the breeze with the scent of waffle cakes, cinnamon-baked apples, hot dogs, cotton candy and beer. It was an interesting mix and fairly shouted festival, Lane thought as she moved to the edge of her porch.

All the narrow roads in Old Town had been blocked and cleared of traffic, and throngs of people danced in the streets in the chilly night air. Police officers were everywhere, and men like Tyler stood in fluorescent orange vests holding flashlights to direct visitors. It looked like fun. *He* looked like fun.

No, she corrected. He looked like an ad for the "manly" things: beer, cigars, power tools and big trucks. Tyler in black jeans and a leather bomber jacket that was so worn it was almost beige brought butterflies to her stomach that refused to settle. Tyler in a suit gave him the James Bond look and made her heart skip a couple of beats. What would Tyler in nothing do to her?

Instead of telling herself no, instead of reminding herself that she couldn't have a relationship with someone with the notoriety Tyler gained, she let her mind break free and imagine his naked body. He was all lean muscle and smooth, tanned skin, maybe a couple of scars…a really tight behind….

As if sensing her, he looked back over his shoulder. His smile fell slowly and even from the distance between her porch and the street, she could see his eyes darken. He knew what she was thinking! She blushed furiously and understood that his thoughts weren't far from hers. Now the warning that this was dangerous ground pulsed through her brain. Still, when he waved her over to him, she went.

"Hi," he said softly.

She stared up at him, light from the antique street lamp gleaming over his dark hair. "Hi yourself." Her heart thumped being near him, and though she wasn't a small woman, she suddenly felt delicate and vulnerable.

"Were you here last year for this?" he asked.

"Yes, but I'd only just opened the shop. I don't think half the town even knew the bookstore was here."

He hadn't known she was here, either, Tyler thought, smiling down at her as she looked out over the crowd across the street. People danced where they stood or danced down the street.

"Dance with me."

She tensed and Tyler noticed. "I really need to get back to the shop," she said.

"Lock it up and put the Closed sign in the window."

"Tyler, I'm running a business."

"Who's going to shop for books while all this is going on?" He gestured at the vendor wagons, the dancers, the sparkling lights.

That was true. "I do need to take Peggy more supplies. She's manning my vendor wagon."

Tyler smiled to himself. Lane had to have an excuse to have fun. "Then get them and we'll go."

"Aren't you on duty?"

"Yeah, but that doesn't mean I can't have fun, too. Go on, go." He turned to give directions to a festival goer as Lane hurried back into the store. She returned shortly with a box of coffee supplies and wearing her jacket. Signaling to the next man stationed a little farther down the street, Tyler removed the safety vest and stuffed it in his pocket, then took the box from Lane.

They made their way through the crowd, and in a few minutes reached Peggy and the vendor wagon, both beneath a spreading oak tree. An attractive young man was perched on the flagstone wall that curved along the waterfront.

Peggy handed a customer a latte and looked at Lane. "Hi, Miss Lane. Hey, big brother," Peggy said.

Lane swung her gaze to Tyler. "Brother?"

He shrugged, setting the box near Peggy. "I've

known Peggy since she was born,'' he explained. ''Her oldest brother, Jace, is my age.''

Lane blinked. ''Whoa, small-town life must agree with Diana,'' Lane said. ''She doesn't look old enough to have a son your age.''

''Mom and Dad married right out of high school. Mom put Dad through college,'' Peggy said. Tyler remained silent, glowering at the young man sitting near them, and Peggy sent him a wide-eyed ''Would you please stop staring, you're embarrassing me'' look. He didn't oblige her. Lane could almost see the kid sweating under Tyler's regard.

''Dad says he'd never have amounted to anything if Mom hadn't been with him,'' Peggy added. ''This is Dean Parker. He's a senior at the University of South Carolina.''

Lane shook his hand. ''Nice to meet you.''

Tyler just stared at him.

Lane nudged him and he scowled at her. ''Lighten up, will you?'' she said softly, and he shook the young man's hand. ''Why don't you take a break?'' Lane said. ''I'll cover you for a bit.''

''Are you sure? What about the shop?''

''Closed it. As Tyler pointed out, who's going to shop for books on a night like this?''

''You sure?''

''Of course. Go on. Nice to meet you, Dean,'' Lane said.

''Thank you, ma'am,'' Dean said, and glanced briefly at Tyler.

The couple walked away, hand in hand.

''Don't go far,'' Tyler called.

"Tyler! For pity's sake, she's nineteen, a grown woman not a child," Lane said.

"And he's a man. I know how they think." Tyler was still scowling at Peggy and Dean's backs.

"Well, I don't think Dean'll do anything after the way your eyes drilled a hole in him."

"He looks unsavory."

Lane found this highly amusing. Tyler was like a father defending his daughter against all hormone-challenged males. "Because he wears an earring?"

"Partly."

"My brother wears an earring."

He lifted a brow at that.

"And Peggy told me Dean's got a full scholarship. I doubt if he's any kind of slacker." Lane's lips quirked. "It's not like they just met, you know."

"I've never seen him before."

"And you're privy to everything in her life?"

"Yeah, just about. She's like one of my sisters."

"Peggy and Dean have both been away at school together. They've been dating for a year now."

"I didn't know that. How do you know?"

"Peggy told me. She worked for me for a couple of days before tonight. And unlike you, I haven't had my head buried in files and corporate meetings despite what the gossip says."

"I thought you didn't listen to gossip."

"Doesn't mean I don't hear it."

He sighed and took Dean's seat on the stone wall. "Yeah, I have been working a lot. Until lately."

"Are you going to blame me for that?"

"Well, you *are* a task."

"Really?" she said, pursing her lips.

Tyler smiled as he watched Lane serve a couple of customers, then took the latte she prepared for him. He stayed where he was and turned his gaze to the crowd. There were vendors from every store, and the local radio station was covering the event. Tyler returned his gaze to Lane. She was moving fast and furiously now, and when he asked if she needed help, she waved him off, claiming to be "in the zone." Still he watched her, his imagination coming quickly into play.

The party lights shone down on her, turning her hair the color of autumn leaves, but it was the light that lined the walkway that offered him the silhouette of her long legs beneath her skirt. He remembered seeing her running on the beach. He hadn't known it was her at first. She'd been right, it was too dark. But when she'd walked up the beach path between the properties, he knew. No one had posture that straight. Regal. She didn't walk into a room, she glided. And he'd bet his inheritance that there was a lot more beneath those layers of clothes and ugly hairdos that she would ever show anyone.

He wanted her to show it to him.

He realized it wasn't just a sexual attraction—though there was that, and if he thought about their last kiss, he wouldn't be able to stand straight—but the attraction was her quick mind, her wit. And that she wouldn't open up to anyone. She let a person get so far, then closed the door. Tyler liked pushing against it.

"What's your brother's name?"

She looked up, surprised. "Oh, ah, Angel."

"Strange name for a guy."

"It's a nickname for Angelo."

"Angelo Douglas, hmm?"

"How about your brothers and sisters?" she said quickly.

"There are four of us. You met my brother Kyle, and between us is Reid. And we have one sister, Kate. Kate's married with children."

"And did you drill a hole in her husband the way you did Dean?"

"I whipped the tar out of him once."

Lane whirled, her eyes wide. "You what?"

"We were in high school. He hit on my prom date."

"Oh." Lane managed a smile, but Tyler saw a little sadness behind it.

Lane envied that he'd grown up around the same people all his life. She couldn't recall anyone from her childhood that she wasn't related to.

"Any more siblings?" he asked her.

"Richard, Mark and Sophie." At least, those were the anglicized versions. She wanted to say to him, *I'm Elaina, Elaina Honora Giovanni.* Her grandmother's name was Douglas, the Irish half of her bloodline.

Lane served customers and handed over the reins to Peggy when she returned. Dean got behind the cart with her, helping, and Lane had to pull Tyler away. "Come on, watchdog," she said. Tyler tossed his coffee cup in the trash and in one smooth move swung Lane into his arms and into a dance.

"Tyler, what are you doing?" she asked, embarrassingly out of step, whatever the dance was.

"The shag."

"I beg your pardon?"

She must have attended boarding schools, he thought. Her diction was always perfect, just like her posture.

"It's easy. You're not a real Southerner if you can't shag," he said.

"Apparently." Around them the laughter and excitement of the crowd grew. It was infectious.

"Loosen up, Lane, you're stiff as a board."

"Why, thank you, Fred Astaire." She tried, honestly she did, and it took another song for her to learn the steps, and then she was having fun. Her father used to tell her brothers that the man who can dance gets the girls. And Tyler must have stolen them all. He was a great lead, and for a moment, the area cleared for them. He spun her, dipped, with a little samba, and Lane didn't care that the crowd had singled them out. Her head was spinning as fast as Tyler could spin her in the dance steps. People sang with the band. Flashbulbs blinked in the night. The flicks of bright light made her flinch and she missed a step but Tyler pulled her close and then the rest of the world didn't matter.

Tyler felt her laughter sing through him. Once she got the hang of the dance, she was wild, and he wished the music wouldn't stop. Beach music. A chilly night, a bonfire. He was inside a little slice of heaven.

Then the song ended, people applauded, and Lane buried her face in his chest, catching her breath.

"Oh, that was fun!" she said, tipping her head back to look at him. "Thank you."

He grinned, pushing hair off her cheek. "Been a while since you cut loose?"

"Yeah, I guess." She'd nearly forgotten she could let go like that. She'd been hiding, careful for so long.

"Come on, I have to get back to my post till midnight. Unless you'd like to stay behind?"

"No, I'll go back with you."

His heart squeezed when she moved close to him and didn't stiffen when he put his arm around her. They walked back toward her shop, the crowd thinning now, and Tyler sat on her porch steps with her.

"Want more coffee?" she asked.

"No thanks, I'm wired for sound now."

"A beer, wine?"

He tipped an imaginary cap. "Can't. I'm on duty, ma'am."

Lane leaned back against the porch rail, a couple of feet separating them as he did the same. "Thank you, Tyler."

"For what?"

"Making me an official Southerner."

He winked at her. "You'll have to work on the drawl, though. We could do it again at the Winter Ball, at the end of festival week."

He could almost see the door slam shut. "Thanks for asking, but I can't."

"Why not?"

"A gentleman is not supposed to question a lady's refusal."

He made a face. "You went to charm school or something, didn't you?"

"My mother was a stickler for being proper."

"Well, that's hooey."

"Hooey?"

"Yeah, baloney, unfounded, nothing—hooey."

"Do you know how silly you sound?"

"I don't care. Why not go with me?"

"I think people will get the wrong idea about us if I do."

"And what idea is that?"

"That we're together."

"We haven't really been together yet."

In the dark she turned red, heat spreading up her face.

"But we will be," he said.

"See? That's where the bad reputation comes in, Tyler. You assume too much. I'm not going to sleep with you."

"I hadn't planned on sleeping with you at all."

Her momentum dropped.

"I'd planned on doing everything in bed with you but sleep."

Lanes insides ignited. His words set off a waterfall of sensation—hot, molten, earth-shaking power moving through her body, under her skin, to land in a spot between her thighs. She was suddenly very warm and damp at the thought of him touching her, of being in a big bed and doing as he said…anything but sleeping.

"What if I just don't want to go to the Winter Ball?"

"Then don't."

"Okay, this discussion is over, then."

"Not a chance in hell."

"You'll keep asking?"

"Till you give me a good enough reason to stop."

"I don't have to."

"Yes, you do."

"Why?" she cried.

He slid over till he was right beside her, facing her, his leg cocked and touching hers. "Because you've lived in the town for nearly two years and haven't met anyone but Nalla and a few customers. Because the townspeople all need to see the woman I'm seeing."

Her insides melted.

"And the Winter Ball is like a cotillion. We all dress up and pretend we're high society."

Which was exactly why she didn't want to go. There would be cameras, reporters.

"It's a fun night, like a fairy tale. It gets everyone geared up for Christmas. And if you don't go with me, then I have to go alone," Tyler said.

He was on the city council of aldermen. It was politically correct for him to go.

"You could take another date."

"You want me to?"

"I don't care."

But she did. He could see it in her eyes.

"I'll have to think about it more," she said.

He frowned. "Okay, that's better than a no, I guess."

"I said think, not yes."

"Fair warning," he said, putting up a hand. He stared at her for a second, then settled back on his forearms. "You know, Lane, I've never had to work this hard for a date in my life." He stretched his legs out, his gaze on the crowd, ever vigilant.

"That I do not doubt."

Lane's gaze rode the long-legged length of him, and she felt the quiet power he exuded. It made her hunger to feel his bunching muscles and tanned skin. To feel him moving against her, naked and slow.

"Maybe once before. MarySue Sanford."

Lane blinked, drawn out of her thoughts. "Mary-Sue?"

"Yeah, she had braids and red hair. She didn't want to share my swing with me."

"I can only assume from experience that you badgered her to give in."

His smile was self-deprecating. "She socked me in the eye. Knocked me flat on my back."

Lane laughed. She could see it, Tyler staring up at an angry redhead telling him, "Boys are stupid."

"Must be the red hair," he said, and she elbowed him.

"Do you always think you're going to get everything you want?"

He thought about that. "If I didn't, I wouldn't go after anything at all. My mom says I'm like a terrier with a bone. I refuse to give up. Just so you know that."

She rolled her eyes. "Gee. Thanks for the news flash. I'm flattered, Tyler."

He made a face. "I don't want you to be flattered. I want you to give in." He pushed himself up slightly, leaning as he did, his intent to kiss her clear to anyone who was watching.

"And then what?"

He stilled, halfway to his target. "Then what, what?"

"Then what happens? Suppose you have me, Tyler, we share some fun, a bed. Then what?"

"I'm not looking for a lifetime commitment, Lane."

Her brows drew down. "So all this pursuing is for the Winter Ball? For a dance?"

He sat up, his gaze probing, and she wondered what or who he was dissecting—himself or her? "No. Of course not."

A calm settled over her and she sighed against the post, staring out into the street. People milled past, searching for their cars and home.

"Me, neither. And I told you before, I'm not prepared to be the talk of the town, one of your conquests, and then be left to gather up the pieces. Trust me when I say I've been there, done that."

She stood and walked to the door, unlocking it.

"Lane?"

"Good night, Tyler."

He was still staring at the door when the lock snicked and the lights went off.

Well, dang, he thought. Now what?

Nalla Campanelli was an exquisitely beautiful woman. She didn't work very hard to be so, a fact that was irritating to half the females in the town. Lane admired Nalla for her approach to life, which was full throttle. She was as comfortable in a power suit as she was in denim cutoffs and a tank top. Though her restaurant was small, it was on the newly renovated waterfront. Prime real estate and her customers came for the spectacular view and the comfortable atmosphere. You could have a quiet, elegant four-course meal in the Cracked Crab on the upper level, or you could make a complete pig of yourself and a huge mess smacking soft-shelled crabs with a mallet at the ground floor tables. The restaurant was an extension of Nalla, both elegant and laid-back.

It was closed now, but after hours was when Lane got to try the latest additions to the menu. Now she was tasting the puff pastry.

"I know you'll tell me honestly." Nalla twirled her long braid of bright red hair, then tossed it over her shoulder.

"Too much salt. It's not enhancing the pastry, it's overpowering it."

Nalla nodded, making a note in a big binder. "The filling?"

"Sorry, all I can taste is salt."

"Okay, tomorrow I'll give it another try before I put it on the menu."

"I'm going to be huge if we keep this up," Lane said.

"You're the only one who'll tell me the truth. My staff thinks I'll fire them if they don't like my creations."

Nalla opened a bottle of wine, filled two goblets and handed one to Lane. "Let's go upstairs. The breeze is great this time of day."

Lane followed Nalla. They'd just settled on the porch on the upper level when Nalla said, "So tell me about Tyler."

"Should I ask about Kyle?"

Nalla looked at her wineglass, then propped her bare feet on the rail. "Maybe another time, okay?"

It must really hurt, Lane thought. Nalla was usually open about her emotions. "Tyler is in hot pursuit and he won't take no for an answer. He wants to take me to the Winter Ball."

"Do you want to say no?"

"Of course not. But not only is he not looking for a lasting relationship, I can't risk Dan Jacobs or any other reporter finding me, and Tyler McKay dines with the governor. And Dan's been paid for a story he didn't finish. That makes him dangerous. He and every other reporter like him want more. My father is the only one who knows where I am, and I made him swear himself to secrecy."

"I say you should confess to him. Tyler would protect you."

"But I've been lying to him and he hates lies."

"No, you're protecting yourself. There's a difference. Once Tyler knows the awful things Dan Jacobs did, I bet he goes charging off to defend your honor."

"I can't count on that. I don't know how he'd react to the truth about my identity."

"You falling for this guy, aren't you, Elaina?"

It felt good to have someone call her by her real name. "I think so."

"Do you want to sleep with him?"

She remembered what Tyler had said about no sleeping at all. "Oh, yeah."

"Maybe it isn't the press-corps threat that's bothering you. If you have Tyler, that means you have to be a part of something, and you've been a part of nothing for so long."

Lane felt tears wet her eyes and she unpinned her hair. The breeze immediately whipped it back. "You can't know what it was like.'' Microphones in her face, flashbulbs popping in her bedroom windows, seeing her photograph in the morning paper....

''You're right, I can only imagine,'' Nalla said. ''You lost everything. The man you thought you loved, your reputation, your showing and the deal with that chain of stores that was going to carry your clothing line—it had to be devastating. But are you prepared to just shut yourself off from the world for the rest of your life? You do, and the media still wins. Dan Jacobs still wins. I say fight back.''

''I tried.'' Whatever she'd said to the press was misconstrued. Dan was one of their own and they were certain he was telling the truth. The fact that she and her father had given the FBI the winery books to prove there wasn't any money laundering didn't make it into the headlines.

''No, I mean, fight for yourself alone, not the career. Not the family. I know you fought for them.''

''And lost.''

''But *you* make the choices now, Elaina, not them. If Dan Jacobs shows up, sic Tyler on him.'' Nalla took a sip of wine and shrugged. ''Heck, sic all the McKays.''

Lane swallowed half her wine in two big gulps. She was tired of lying and hiding. And like Cinderella, she really wanted to go to the ball.

''Just think about it, okay? We still have the Midnight Jubilee, the sailing races, the rodeo out by the Stanley farm, the craft shows, and there's that concert in the park, which is my favorite part of the Winter Festival.''

''Good grief.'' Lane hadn't participated last

year—too busy keeping a low profile—and had forgotten about the events.

"Oh, wait till Jubilee. The street looks like we rolled back time. White lights, carolers, period costumes, and…you need to dress better."

"Excuse me?"

"Way better."

Lane looked down at the rust-colored outfit she was wearing. A good color for her, just too many layers, which had been her intention.

"Come on, Lane. You need to be festive." Excitement sparkled in Nalla's eyes. "This is the prelude to Christmas, and it's like a fantasy. Hors d'oeuvres served in the street by men in livery, shopping, socializing. Parties." Nalla lifted her arms and wiggled in the chair.

Lane considered how festive she needed to get. "What will you be wearing?"

Nalla's smile was slow. "A fabulous, slinky, blue-beaded cocktail dress that I saved for a year to buy."

"A year? It must have cost a fortune. I'd love to see it."

"You have."

Lane's brows drew together.

"It's one of your designs."

Seven

Nalla had been right.

The Midnight Jubilee was like a fantasy.

Much of the historic district had been blocked off. Shops were closed early to be open late until after the concert in the park. During the day, white lights had been strung in the small trees and bushes lining the streets, as well as the lampposts, and shop owners had prepared amazing displays for their windows.

Lane had spent the morning fussing over hers. Her wide windowsills were draped in rippling blue velvet, white lights and glitter displaying the books and other items her shop offered.

As well as adding two more radio spots to the ones she'd already arranged, she'd contracted Nalla to prepare a delicious variety of appetizers. They'd be a draw in themselves, Lane thought. As the other shop owners had done, she'd set up a booth in the street offering free wine and appetizers to the people strolling by. Soft, string music drifted from speakers positioned down Bay Street, and the employees on the street were dressed in period clothing.

At seven, the Antebellum Verder house's magnificent federal staircase would be lined with carolers in period dress, singing for the towns folk. Here they *were* towns folk, she thought as she swept open her doors at sunset and greeted people. The entire area was alive with energy and excitement.

And it didn't take long for Lane's delight to turn to panic.

Who'd have thought there would be so many people? She attributed it to the author who was signing her latest novel and who knew just about everyone that walked through the door. The woman assured Lane she could manage on her own. Lane rushed from the register, to the table of food, to the author. Then she was off to root through stock or shelves to find books for customers. And then there was the coffee bar. The temperature had dropped and people wanted hot cappuccinos and lattes, instead of wine and sodas.

It was a neverending cycle, and Lane was glad she was wearing a shorter skirt and loose jacket tonight. She would have been tripping over her own feet in an ankle-length skirt. She was kicking herself for not hiring help. She'd have at least liked the opportunity to talk to some of these people, instead of racing about.

* * *

Tyler took in the chaos and crowds in the small store.

"My goodness, look at all these people," his sister, Kate, said, coming in behind him.

Startled to see her, he gave her a kiss on the forehead and said, "I bet she didn't expect it." Tyler moved through the crowd toward Lane, who was rushing around and looking a little frazzled.

"Hey, Lane."

She punched numbers on the register and looked up as it spit out a receipt. "Hi." Man, he looked good, she thought, flushing at the sight of him. The blue sweater made his eyes look bluer and his shoulders bigger. And right now, she wanted to lean on them. "Wish I could chat, but..." She bagged the books, added a couple bookmarks, then handed it to her customer. "Thank you. And I'll call you with that book search this week."

She immediately went to the coffee bar and started making coffees for the people lined up at the counter. Tyler's gaze shifted to the customers headed for the register, to the author, the food table and the young woman who was obviously looking for her.

"Uh-oh," Tyler said, inclining his head to his sister. He hurried over to Lane.

"Need some help?"

"No, yes—I'll get back to you on that."

Tyler slipped behind the counter and grabbed mugs and napkins for her as she assembled the different coffees. "I'm capable and my sister is here."

Her head jerked up. "Your sister!"

The dark-haired woman smiled. Lane instantly saw the resemblance. "Hi, I'm Kate."

Lane blinked at her, working the espresso machine without really having to look. "Hello. It's nice of you to drop by."

"Just what you needed, huh? Another customer?" Kate said with a glance at the packed little shop.

"Amazing, isn't it?" Despite the chaos, Lane was thrilled at the business. But with fans clustered around the author, there was barely room to move.

"We can pitch in, you know," Kate offered.

"Oh, no, I couldn't ask you to—"

"We offered," Tyler said. "Why didn't you hire Peggy?"

"I didn't think it would be so busy. Not like this." She waved at the people. "Peg is out there somewhere, enjoying the festival with Dean."

"Well, I can run one of these," Kate said, gesturing at the espresso machine.

"You can? Oh, thank heaven…"

Tyler leaned close and put his hand at the small of Lane's back. The instant he touched her, the tension started slipping away and Lane let out a tired breath.

"Let us help," he said softly. "We want to. Besides, all anyone can do out there is shop." He made a face. "Not my top fun thing at any hour."

Lane looked up at him, so grateful she felt her eyes burn.

Kate moved behind the counter, pushing Tyler away and grabbing an apron with the shop's name, A Novel Idea, printed across the front.

"You're sure?" Lane said to her. "This isn't how you meant to spend your evening."

"No, I could be chasing after my kids, who are

likely driving their father crazy. Then it would be home to do laundry, dishes and try to get the kids to bed. All that, or here, making coffee? Gee, what a choice.'' She flashed a smile.

Lane still looked doubtful.

''I did this for a couple of years while I was in school and then in college,'' Kate assured her, and Lane smiled her thanks and went to the register, forgetting Tyler.

He watched her move around the store, smiling, laughing with people, bringing a fresh drink to the author.

''She seems nice, Ty.'' Kate finished making the coffee and change for the customer, then started on the next one.

''If she lets her guard down long enough to show you,'' Tyler said.

''Oh, my, dissecting already. A good sign.''

His gaze snapped to his little sister. As she did in her own kitchen, she moved like lightning. ''You're going to give me an opinion after just meeting her?''

''Sorta. Mom and Diana like her. She's not like that witch you used to be tangled up with.''

Grinning, Tyler gave Kate a quick hug. She might be small, but she was a dragon when it came to her family. Clarice was lucky to have left town before Kate got to her.

''I know she's not, peanut.''

Kate leaned close to be heard over the frothing steam. ''But?'' she prodded. ''I know there's a but coming. There always is with you, Ty.''

''But she's hiding something, I can feel it.''

''Married?''

"No, but there's something about her that almost feels familiar." He'd just noticed that. Tonight she wasn't covered with long skirts and big sweaters, and as his gaze followed her, he admired the body wrapped in the stylish suit. Her skirt met the edge of a long, knee-length jacket in black-and-gold tapestry. The high stand-up collar and frothy-looking white blouse made it look almost like a period costume. It was—what was the word? Trendy. And not something he'd have thought Lane would own. But man, he thought, look at those legs.

Kate peered over the counter at Lane, then shrugged. "Take it slow, except for right now. Why don't you go see if you can help? Oh, look there's Mom and Kyle."

Tyler groaned and headed them off before they could get to Lane. His mother had spies and no doubt she'd known about every time he'd been with Lane. He didn't want Lane feeling pressured, and the McKays had a way of laying it on a bit thick sometimes.

"Well, this is interesting," his mother said, giving him a look that reminded him of when he was a teenager and came in drunk after a football game and tried to hide it.

"Gimme a break, Mom."

"Why are you so defensive?" Kyle asked.

"Half my family's in this store checking out a woman I'm seeing, and you ask that?"

"We're shopping." His mother smiled and Tyler knew it was a lie.

When a customer asked him a question about a book, Tyler glanced around, saw that Lane was still frantic and said, "Let me see if I can find it." He gestured for the woman to step ahead of him, then paused to look at his mother.

"She's doing this alone, so if you want to pry, lend a hand, please."

Then he moved off, searching the shelves for the novel the woman was insisting would just tear his heart out. Then why read it? he wondered. He knew what having his heart torn out felt like already.

Lane glanced up to see Tyler's mother, of all people, serving punch and hors d'oeuvres. Mortified, she excused herself and rushed over.

"Mrs. McKay, I can take that." She went to take the tray.

The older woman held it out of her reach. "I told you to call me Laura, and I'm doing fine. I waited tables once, you know. At a Huddle House."

"Really?" Lane couldn't imagine the elegant woman serving in a roadside waffle restaurant.

Laura leaned close. "I got fired after the third day. Apparently I wasn't destined for greatness and they noticed. But I think after waiting on my children for years, I can manage this."

"I'm horrified you're doing this, you know."

Laura laid her hand on Lane's arm. "Honey, you need some help. Accept it. Besides, it's fun. It's not all that often I get to play hostess."

"If you're sure," Lane said, deeply touched by all the help.

"Go on, do the things no one else can." She nodded to the register.

Lane hesitated, then gave up, heading to help another customer.

Three hours later, the author's latest release was sold out, Laura McKay had invited her to a family barbecue after the charity football game tomorrow, which Tyler was playing in, and Kate's husband had shown up with sleepy children in his arms and cotton candy stuck in his hair.

Lane fell into the stuffed chair and kicked off her shoes.

"Bravo," Tyler said, sitting across from her.

"I'm wiped out."

"Great night, huh?"

"Oh, yeah. I'm stunned, absolutely shell-shocked." She'd do something nice for Laura and Kate for all their help. While Laura had left after the author had, Kate had hung around. Tyler's sister was funny and bright, and they'd become fast friends already. It wasn't hard to like a McKay, that was for sure.

Tyler moved to the edge of the chair and grasped Lane's ankle, lifting it to his lap.

"Tyler—"

"Hush up, and relax," he ordered, kneading her foot. She moaned tiredly, closing her eyes, and Tyler brought her other foot to his lap and lavished attention on it.

She started to protest again, then gave up and enjoyed the intense relief. She'd been doing that a lot lately—giving up when a McKay was around. They were a pretty persuasive bunch. Tyler's hands were strong, sending currents up her legs and making her spine liquefy. She sank deeper into the chair.

"I really need to clean up." She didn't have to look to know her store was a mess.

When she tried to pull her feet free, he gripped them tighter. "Save it for the morning. The night isn't over."

"It is for me."

"There's the concert."

"I'll pass, but thank you."

"I have a blanket and a spot picked out."

She opened her eyes and he gave her such an adorably wishful smile that Lane felt herself sinking. Then his hands moved higher on her legs, and Lane experienced a hot rush of need that shot like a bolt right to her center. Low in her stomach, desire simmered as his hands moved upward under her skirt hem.

"Tyler. Are you trying to feel me up?"

He smiled, something taking flight inside him just then. "I'm not trying. You have great legs, darlin'." He leaned forward in the chair, letting her feet slide to the floor as his hands moved farther up her thighs.

"They go all the way up," she said, and wondered why she wasn't warning him off, protesting. But she knew. She was falling hard for him, and when his hand shifted under her hem, she only wanted him to touch her.

"Come here," he said and Lane sat up.

Tyler felt his insides tighten. Little things from Lane meant a lot, he realized, and he wanted to get inside her head, explore who she was under that reserved exterior. He suspected she was hiding a lot of fire, too, and he brushed her mouth with his, coaxing it out.

A little sound escaped her and he swallowed it. She let her hands hover over his thighs, wanting to touch and knowing it was a step forward. Her hesitation strung him tighter, and the minute her palms flattened on his thighs, a hard jolt of desire shot through him. It left him trembling and greedy for her.

"Oh, man," he said, and sank into her mouth. His tongue speared between her lips. Her fingertips dug into his thighs. Her breathing grew labored and Tyler felt like a simmering kettle about to boil over. He gripped her waist and was about to pull her onto his lap when the phone rang.

Lane jerked back, gasping for air, then seemed to glare at the office in the back. "I need to get that."

She rose and headed to the office.

Tyler flopped back into the chair, closing his eyes for a second and reliving the last moments. He was hard, ready to make love to her. It was a frequent occurrence when he was near her, and he didn't think he'd ever wanted a woman more.

The sound of her voice drifted to him in the quiet shop, a soft hum on the air, and something about it made him frown. He stood, moving toward the back of the shop. The door to her office was ajar and he could see her.

And hear her. Speaking fluent Italian.

That sent him back a step, and though he couldn't understand a word, he could tell she was angry at the caller. Her temper was incredible. Who'd have thought? She'd never lost it with him, even when he'd given her a reason. But here she was, rubbing her forehead, gesturing wildly with her free hand.

Whoever was on the other end of the line was getting scorched.

Lane listened to her father. "No, Papa, I can't just

walk right back into my old life. It's over.'' They'd
had this same conversation off and on for nearly two
years now.

''*Mio cuore*, no. That's not so.''

Her throat tightened. It had been difficult to admit
that her career, her name, had been destroyed in one
fell swoop. Surely even her father had to see it would
take more than coming back and picking up her
drawing pencils.

''Until Angel stops hanging out with those men,
goes to the FBI and tells them what he knows about
any deals he's been hatching, I won't even consider
coming back. I don't *want* to come back,'' she said.

''You cannot tell me you are happy in that little
town.''

She glanced toward the partially open doorway
and imagined Tyler beyond it. ''Today, yes, very.''

''You're give up designing forever?''

''I can't predict the future, Papa. But Dan Jacobs
is looking for me—you said so yourself last time you
called that he's still prying.''

''But the talk has died.''

''And coming back will bring it up again. I'm not
ready to fight that.'' Her eyes burned and she rubbed
her forehead again, pain drilling a hole in the back
of her skull. If he kept saying the same things each
time he called, why did he bother? Didn't he remember the photos in the tabloids of her in various states
of dress, the panic and stress when her show fell into
ruin? Or the horrible things they'd said about him?
Even the transcript of her sister's divorce hearing
was printed!

''Angelo is sorry.''

"Angel isn't sorry for anyone but himself, Papa. Is he being hounded by reporters, too?"

"His new friends keep them away."

"I'll bet. What is he doing gambling in Vegas with those…hoods?"

Bastian Giovanni released a long sigh and Lane could imagine him reaching for the bowl of wine corks and fiddling with them. He always toyed with them when he was frustrated. "He won't tell me. He says they are just friends, nothing more. He keeps asking me to trust him."

"And you are. Don't deny it, if he were my child, I'd probably give him the benefit of the doubt first, too." She looked at the door. "I have to go, Papa, I have a guest."

"A man? Make nice with him. You need to give me grandchildren, Elaina."

She smiled. "You want to tell me exactly what 'making nice' means again, Papa?"

He tisked softly and she knew his mood was lightening. "Such sarcasm from my favorite child."

Lane closed her eyes. "I have to go. I love you, Papa."

"I love you, too, my heart," he said.

"And, Papa?"

"Yes?"

"Please don't badger me about coming home. I've been getting enough badgering lately," she said with a glance toward the door. "And this is my home now." She heard her father's long-suffering sigh before he agreed and hung up.

Lane put the phone back in the cradle, her fingers

trailing over it. She missed him. She missed her brothers and sister.

Lane rejoined Tyler in the shop. "I'm sorry about that."

"Don't be. I didn't know you could speak Italian so well."

Panic shot across her face. "Do *you?*"

"Not a word."

Her shoulders sagged with relief. "One of those boarding schools was in Italy," she said.

It wasn't a lie. She'd spend summers at home with her father, but school was a different story. Papa had always been busy with the winery, and her mother had been just plain busy.

"Want to go to the concert?" he asked. "It's about to start."

"I don't think I'm up to it."

"Well, it looks like that phone call didn't go well, so why not? The concert will take your mind off it."

Lane met his gaze, and inside, her emotions yanked up a ladder she wasn't ready to climb. How could her father think she'd return when Dan Jacobs was so intent on finding her that he'd gone to Italy to hound her father? What did Dan want from her? He'd already taken away everything she'd loved. No, she couldn't go back, even if talk died. She was just too weary of it all.

Lane wasn't even aware that Tyler had maneuvered her to the staircase leading to her apartment above until the lock clicked closed.

He handed her the keys. She looked around. He'd locked all the doors, lights were out.

"I have to watch you all the time, don't I?" she said.

He smiled. "I wish you would." He opened the door to the mudroom, which was now her private foyer, and nudged her toward the polished, curved staircase. "I know when I'm beat. You're practically asleep right now."

"I can manage the rest alone."

"I know you can. I'm walking you up to the door."

Lane shook her head, climbing the staircase and feeling every minute of the day in the cells of her body. They were screaming for a hot bath and sleep.

At the top landing, Tyler looked around. There was a small sitting area at the end of the hall near a window, plants hiding the view from the street. There had once been four separate rooms up here. Now the walls on one side of the hall had been knocked out, opening the areas for living, dining and a small kitchen. It was furnished like something out of a magazine. Rich fabrics draped the windows and pooled on the floor, and there were wrought-iron fixtures, as well as crystal, and antiques rested alongside polished oak tables. Everything was textured, overstuffed, designed for comfort.

The apartment looked lived in and cozy.

"I like this," he said. "You interested in doing up my place?"

Lane smiled and sagged against the wall. "No. Go home, Tyler."

"Not going to show me around?"

"Living room, dining room, kitchen, bedroom,

guest room," she said pointing sluggishly in the general direction.

He chuckled and stepped close. "Aren't you glad tomorrow is Sunday?

"Thrilled beyond belief." Today had been more tiring than a design show. And those had been nuts.

"Are you going to the sailing races tomorrow?"

"Gee, not on my to-do list."

"Kyle and I are sailing."

"Why doesn't that surprise me?"

"It's a tradition. McKays have been in every regatta since the first one. We've never actually *won* a race, but we've been there."

He was inches from her, and as tired as she was, a part of Lane was screaming for his attention. "You want me to come watch you sail? Is this like watching a jock practice football?"

He brushed the back of his hand lightly across her cheek. "Sorta." Her hair had come undone and was falling around her shoulders. It was glorious, deep, blood-red fire, and the sight of it turned him on.

"You have enough groupies."

"Do not."

"Not enough groupies? Or no groupies at all?" she countered.

He had to think for a second and she laughed lightly.

"Neither," he said. "Because you're the only one who matters."

"This week."

He reared back, searching her features, her eyes. "If you think that's the case, Lane, then we need to get better acquainted.'' He paused and then in a hurt voice said, ''You really believe that?''

''I've been trying hard to.'' She sighed and something inside her conceded another battle. She was really hopeless when it came to this man. ''You're not an easy guy to resist, Tyler McKay.''

He insinuated his knee between her thighs and pressed her to the wall. ''Then stop trying.''

His mouth was on hers before she could speak, taking, nibbling, the power of the kiss growing stronger by the second. Her insides unwound and she felt as if she was melting into the floor. So she gripped his waist, pulling him till he mashed her to the hard surface. His mouth was everywhere, on her face, her lips, her throat. And when he dipped lower, Lane didn't stop him.

A button flipped open, then another. A second later his mouth was roaming the swells of her breasts. He left a damp, tingling path behind, and Lane gasped for air, wanting to rip the blouse and bra off and experience his mouth all over her.

''I want you,'' he said against her skin, then again on her mouth. ''I want you badly.''

''Tyler.''

He met her gaze, pushing her hair back. ''I know. I know you're not ready. For that. But damn, Lane, I need to touch you.'' His mouth closed over hers, tongue sweeping the hollow darkness, and Lane answered him. Nipping his lips and running her hand down his chest and inside his jacket.

His hand slid down her hip, her thigh, then curled behind her knee and moved upward, taking the skirt with it. He never stopped kissing her, and her mind went blank to the sensations pelting her like hot rain. He squeezed her thigh, and his knee spread her thighs a little wider. When his fingers met the top of one of her stockings, he drew back, arching a brow.

"You're just full of surprises," he said. She wore stockings and a garter belt. He bet it was black and shifted his hand past, his fingertips brushing her center. The warmth of her nearly undid him.

Desire rocketed through her, weakening her resolve. And a little sound escaped her. Then his name, softly tumbling from her lips.

Then Tyler whispered huskily, "I can feel your heat." His breath was hot near her ear, and his words and touch suspended her on some cliff, teetering. "Do you know what that does to me?"

He ground against her so that she understood. Lane's heart shot to her throat as she ploughed her fingers into his hair and gave back.

He hooked the leg of her panties, his fingertips running slowly under the edge, from her behind over her hip, toward the heat of her. It was more erotic than anything she'd ever experienced. A slow temptation. But she knew Tyler—he was a gentleman. He wouldn't do anything unless she wanted him to. The simple touch was asking a question.

"Open for me, darlin'," he whispered against her mouth.

And a heartbeat later, she did.

Eight

Tyler's heart was pounding so hard it hurt. The rushing sound of his blood filled his ears, yet he understood that this moment crossed a delicate road with Lane. A road he didn't think twice about taking. He was connected to this woman, and the way his heart and mind reacted to her warned him that when he fell, he might never get back up again. She was in the blood pounding through his veins, in the thoughts careering though his mind when he slept, when he worked. And that she was in his arms, willingly and waiting for his touch, shredded everything keeping him from wanting more than this moment.

She twisted against him, his hand lying warmly low on her belly, his fingertips beneath the edge of her silk panties. He dipped and brushed over her center, and her kiss grew stronger.

She shifted, straddled his thigh, her skirt hiked and her body open. And he realized he was trembling a little. He broke the kiss, staring into her eyes.

She whispered his name, a sharp edge to it, pleading.

He slid his finger smoothly over her heat, and her eyes slammed shut. Her moan was low and rough, unlike the Lane he knew. The Lane who'd hide everything from him and the world beyond. She wasn't that woman anymore, and he wanted to touch and taste and be inside her. He parted her, dipping a finger inside. Finding her slick and hot, he groaned. He pushed deeper and she gasped. He stroked his finger in and out and she clawed at his shoulders.

"I love what you do to me," she whispered.

Tyler gave, ignoring the hard throb in his groin and pleasured her, watching her features, feeling every pulse of her skin beneath his fingertips. He was aware of her every nuance, her scent, in more ways than he'd been with any other woman before. She tipped her head back and swallowed rapidly, licking lips swollen from his kiss. Her features were smooth, patient, as the sensations came to her. She rushed nothing, not even this, and caught a rhythm with his touch. It was primal, erotic, and when her hand lowered to the front of his trousers, molding the shape of him, Tyler nearly took her to the floor, he wanted to be inside her so badly. Instead, he pushed deeper, blocking any thought except one from her mind. Pleasure.

His own arousal grew painful as he watched her rise to the summit, and when he circled the bead of her sex, he whispered in her ear. "Let me see you find it. Look at me, baby."

Meeting his gaze, she gripped his shoulders, fingers sliding up his neck, then into his hair as he played her body. He plunged and stroked and she met and took, and he saw the flare of her eyes, heard her breath skip once, twice, then lock in her lungs. He smiled softly, as her feminine muscles flexed wildly. He kissed her and she released the trapped breath, trembling in his arms.

She whimpered tightly, again and again as her climax took her somewhere he wanted to go, and he whispered, "Take it all, all." And held her tightly till she sagged against him.

"No more."

"There's always more." He stroked the sensitive bead at her center and she shivered against him.

She laughed shortly. "Oh, goody."

"That was incredible to see," he said, his arousal pulsing for release he wouldn't take. Not tonight.

She buried her face in the curve of his neck, embarrassed. "I can't believe we did that."

"I can. You finally let me in."

Her head jerked up and she met his gaze.

"I don't know why you hide yourself, Lane, but I see it."

His words should have warned her, but she ignored the warning, trying to catch her breath and still sinking down to earth on a soft cloud.

"And instead of my dreams haunting me with what making love to you might be like, I have that to keep me company."

She blinked. "You dream of me. Of us?"

"Oh, yeah. It was bad before. Now it's going to be torture."

Lane didn't think she could be more stunned. Or more pleased. She'd given him absolutely no reason to think she wanted more, and here he was, making her feel incredibly sexy and wanted. And touching her. Oh, my, the man could touch, she thought, kissing him softly.

Then Tyler lifted her in his arms. She yelped and he kissed her as he carried her into the living room. Gently he laid her on the sofa, making her scoot over so he could sit on the edge. Her expression was clouded, her blouse open, exposing the swell of full breasts. It was another thing she'd hidden. Her body. Tyler knew better now.

"I'm not staying, so get that panicked look off your face," he said.

She arched a brow.

"Don't get me wrong, baby," he said in a low voice. "I want to strip you down to your skin right now and taste every inch of you, but I won't. We won't. Not tonight."

"That implies there'll be another night."

He smiled. "I was hoping you'd caught on to that."

The thought of being naked with Tyler, exploring each other, made her skin grow hot, and she reached for him, latching on to his jacket lapels and pulling him down to her mouth. She kissed him deeply, a sultry darkness sliding between them.

"Go with me to the Winter Ball."

"Ask me in the morning."

"Why?"

"Because right now I'd give you anything."

He smiled against her mouth, his hands swept up her waist, her rib cage, then covered her breasts. She arched into his touch as he maneuvered his hands under her bra and cupped warm skin, still kissing her.

She murmured his name as his fingers circled her nipples. Fire radiated outward, sending signals to her body she couldn't control. She wanted him, right now, and would have bared herself for more if he hadn't eased back.

He stared at her for a long moment. "I have to go." He stood, his desire for her obvious. His hands at his sides, his gaze fixed on the floor. She could hear him breathing slowly.

"Tyler."

"Shh. Don't say anything."

He clenched his hands into fists, struggling between need and common sense. Neither of them was prepared for a night in bed.

Lane would have thought he'd play the cards he held, he held a full house. But he didn't, just stood over her, motionless and breathing hard. She rose, covering herself, then swinging her legs off the sofa.

"I want more from you, Lane," he said softly, "and not just in bed."

For how long? she wondered. When he learned that she'd been lying to him, he'd turn away, she was sure of it. "I can't give you that."

He met her gaze, his blue eyes probing. "I don't know what you're hiding, but it won't make a difference."

Her breath caught for a second. "I'm not hiding anything."

"Liar."

Her eyes flew wide. "How dare you say that!"

"Don't get all indignant. It's true or you'd tell me more about yourself. Tell me who called tonight and upset you, why you spoke in Italian." He shifted, his fingers unfurling. "I could find out on my own, anyway." He saw the panic skate across her features and knew he was right. "But I won't. Because I want you to trust me enough to confide in me."

Lane didn't say anything, because a question or denial would only prove his point. She wasn't ready to trust him that much. Playing with her body was one thing; gambling with her life and privacy was quite another.

"I told you I was patient, Lane," he said, then turned and walked to the hall. She didn't go after him, wisely staying where she was. His footsteps sounded on the staircase, and she heard the door shut softly.

Lane flopped back onto the sofa. Was she ready to trust him? What would his reaction be when he learned she'd lied to him about everything? Having an affair with Tyler McKay sounded great, but she didn't doubt that would be the extent of it. Because though she'd been wounded by Dan Jacobs's betrayal, someone had hurt Tyler. And neither of them was willing to jump into a fire again.

The next morning, Lane managed to drag herself down to the store long enough to clean it, but her thoughts weren't on the incredible profit she'd made last night, but on Tyler and how he'd made her feel, how he'd touched her so intimately.

And how he knew she wasn't telling the truth. She didn't think she could face him without choking on embarrassment after what they'd done. After what he'd done to her. But when she saw the townspeople heading toward the waterfront, she remembered the race. Something inside her egged her on, pushing her to where she was now, staring into her closet. Automatically she reached for the bulky sweaters and skirts, pulling them out... Then she shoved them back, and her hand skimmed to the rear of the closet, to the clothing she'd once designed for a large department-store chain and never got the chance to see worn by other people. Impulse won out over her need to hide.

She couldn't keep doing this, smothering who she was. It was slowly eating at her insides, making her an unlikable person—until Tyler came along. She didn't want to keep being secretive, and though she knew the consequences, she'd take baby steps. Lane studied the clothes, seeking classically conservative, instead of startling. She wasn't ready to show the real Elaina yet. A moment later, she grabbed navy slacks, a striped boat-neck shirt and a canvas windbreaker off the rod.

Now, if she could get to the pier on time to see the start of the regatta...

Tyler glared at Kyle. "I'm trying to feel sympathetic."

"Try harder. I didn't intend to get thrown off the horse, you know."

Kyle had been in the charity rodeo this morning

riding a bronco. He'd been tossed off and landed on his arm, which was now in a cast.

"I know this blows our chances in the race."

Tyler rubbed the back of his neck. "It's not the race, it's the tradition. Without your help, I'm short an experienced deckhand."

"Tyler," Kate said, "I'll sail with you."

Tyler looked at his little sister and smiled tenderly. "Thanks, peanut, but I know how you feel about it. I don't want you scared if it gets hairy out there." Besides, she had a family to think about, and this race was dangerous sometimes.

"Look who I found," a voice called.

Tyler turned, his gaze snapping from his mother to the woman walking beside her. It took a second for recognition to register, and his gaze slid over Lane's body before meeting her gaze. He turned from his siblings and walked toward her. His mother continued on past him to her other children as Tyler stopped, his gaze moving over the slacks that hugged Lane's curves and matched the canvas windbreaker.

"I don't know if I like seeing you dressed like that."

Lane flushed. "How come?"

"Because every man around is going to see what I knew was already there."

"Oh, really?" She felt extraordinarily flattered.

"Yeah, really. Unless they're blind and numb." Her hair was drawn into a ponytail, and he realized it was longer than he'd first thought. And that ponytail made her look fresh and young, and damn sexy. He held her gaze and her hands, leaning forward to brush his mouth over hers. "I thought of you all night," he said.

"You must really be tired, then."

"Nah. Went to sleep with dreams of you shivering in my arms like you did last night."

Heat seeped up her face from her throat. "Tyler, hush. Your family is close enough to hear you." They weren't, but Lane didn't think she could take much more of his pillow talk before she made a fool of herself.

He leaned over, his mouth near her ear. "I look at you and see you like I did then. Damp and incredibly hot. Panting."

Lane felt her heart skip a couple of beats and settle with a slow, hard thud. "Be careful or the whole town's going to know how you feel."

Tyler shifted, his groin responding to her.

She smiled. A smile so sexy and mischievous Tyler felt he'd been let deeper inside her closed world. "I'm glad you came." He glanced back at his brother, then looked at her again. "It might be for nothing, though."

"What's wrong?"

"Kyle broke his arm in the rodeo this morning."

"That's terrible, but why is it a problem for you?"

"He was my partner. I'm short help. Reid's out of town. Kate's afraid of water, though she wouldn't admit to how scared she really is. Mom is…well, too old. It's strenuous."

He turned, wrapping his arm around her waist and leading her to the family. Tyler pulled her down beside him on a wooden trunk on the docks. At their back, the sailboat rocked in the water. The other landings were peppered with entrants readying their crafts.

"How about asking Jace Ashbury?" his mother said.

Tyler shook his head and pointed down two piers to one of his oldest friends. "He's racing this year, too. Ah, well," he said, shrugging and standing. "Might as well shut it down and find a seat in the crowd."

"I'm really sorry, Ty." Kyle apologized again.

"No sweat, it's just a race." Despite his disappointment, Tyler wasn't going to make Kyle feel any worse than he was. Tyler stood up, released Lane and headed to the boat, walking up the plank and dropping onto the deck.

"You really want to do this, don't you," Lane called from the dock.

"It's tradition. A McKay has never missed a race in over a hundred years." Tyler started lashing the sails he'd loosened an hour ago.

Lane felt badly for him. He was trying to hide his disappointment. She looked around in indecision. Who was she to let a tradition die?

"I can sail."

Tyler looked at her, then smiled gently. "It's okay, Lane. It's just a race."

She stepped onto the gangplank, standing halfway between the dock and the boat. "McKay, do you want to sail in this race or not?"

"Yes, but I can't take just anyone as a deckhand. Especially someone who doesn't know how to sail."

"But I *do* know, Captain." Lane pointed to parts of the boat and named them, then to destroy the rest of his doubt, told him which sails she'd work and that the cross wind changed on the river when they met the bridge, so he should be ready for it.

Tyler grinned.

"I think she's serious, Ty," Kyle said from the dock. "I'd take the offer."

Tyler came to the rail, staring into her whiskey-brown eyes. "Why?"

"Because it means so much to you."

Something opened inside him, and he suspected it was the piece of his heart he'd held closed for so long. He smiled and inclined his head for her to come aboard. As she stepped onto the deck, he looked down at her. "Thank you, darlin'." He brushed back a lock of hair that had come loose from the ponytail, watching his moves before meeting her gaze. "Are you ready, Mate?"

"Aye, aye, Captain."

He kissed her quickly, then headed to the bow.

The signal to line up on the water came and they sailed off. Lane's heart pounded, a little sliver of fear working into her. It had been a while since she'd sailed and she didn't want to let Tyler down.

Tyler manned the wheel, the boat engine puttering and taking them to the start line. "You'll have to move fast," he called.

She stood up, her hand on the boom. "Trust me, Tyler. We can do this," she said, and he nodded, his expression serious. She readied herself, and as they approached the line, he cut the engine. The boat rocked as they waited, positioned.

The start gun fired. Tyler unfurled the main sail. The wind, cold and crisp, caught, billowing the bright blue sail, and the boat slid over the water like a razor, gaining speed. Tyler shouted commands and she obeyed. He knew the river and they swept between other boats, neck and neck. It was a fast, hour-long race, the halfway point at the bridge, which was open to accommodate the tall masts. The turnaround just past the bridge would be a telling moment, one that revealed the most likely winner.

Tyler had one of the largest boats, and as she braced her feet and leaned with the heel of the boat, Lane thought he should get a prize for doing this with only the two of them. It was exciting, maddening, and Lane hadn't had this much fun in a long time. They had to make the turnaround quickly, and when she rushed to pull in one sail and let go of another, the boat listed sharply.

"Lane!" Tyler called. "For God's sake, hold on!" She was leaning out over the water, feet braced, rope wrapped in her fists and giving the boat a deep tilt that could put her in the brink.

"I got it!" she yelled. "Just steer!"

He did, his gaze flicking from the open water and her.

"Hey, McKay!" she shouted as the sailboat finished the curve and started to come upright. "Want to win this race?"

Tyler glanced behind, then to her, grinning. "I'll be damned. Come on, baby, let's show them."

They worked in tandem, as if they'd done this a thousand times together. Lane was fast, ducking booms and handling the sheets, stretching her muscles to the limit. The crowd roared, the sound only a growling whisper over the snapping sails and the rush of water.

Another boat pulled alongside them, barely half a length behind. Tyler glanced for a second, then looked at Lane. It was his friend, Jace. Lane took in the sail positions and wind direction for a split second, then pulled the sheet for the main sail. They shot out in front and crossed the finish line a whole length ahead.

The spectators shrieked.

Lane quickly locked down the sail.

Tyler was there, grabbing her in a hard embrace. "We did it! You were magnificent!"

His excitement spilled into her and she leaned back, meeting his gaze. Her smile was bright. "Nothing like breaking a bad streak, huh?"

"Thanks, Lane." He kissed her hard, and when he finally drew back, she was breathless, the chill leaving her skin.

"You sailed, too, you know."

"Yeah, but that last minute there, I thought Jace would take us."

Jace sailed past, saluting them, and Tyler waved, grinning hugely. He looked down at Lane, ridiculously pleased she'd helped him.

"It's a new day, you know."

"Yes," she said warily. *Ask me tomorrow,* she'd said last night.

"Come to the Winter Ball with me."

She stared up at him and couldn't disappoint him. He was so happy right now, and she wanted so much to shed the skin she'd been hiding in for so long and be who she really was. Tyler had peeled away layers and liked what he saw, and that gave Lane the confidence she needed.

"Yes, I'll go with you."

He grinned, a sappy smile. "Good. It's formal, remember."

"I think I can manage to scrounge up something suitable."

He pressed his forehead to hers. "Thanks, baby. What do you say we dock this thing and enjoy our new celebrity status."

Lane paled and her smile disintegrated. She looked down at the dock before he'd notice. Oh, no. She'd forgotten that the winner would be in the papers.

Front page. Statewide.

Wonderful. And when he let her go to secure the craft, she looked toward the pier. The press was already running to the end of the docks to the slip.

How was she supposed to hide from that without hurting Tyler?

Nine

Lane had turned her face away from the camera and hoped Tyler didn't notice. She answered a couple of questions from reporters, but when they got personal, she'd slipped from Tyler's side to let the town golden boy have his limelight. It wasn't every day someone broke a hundred-year-old losing streak.

While the press snapped pictures, Lane headed toward home, only to be called back into the McKay fold by his mother. And sister and brother. Then Tyler. It was clear she wasn't getting out of joining them for the charity football game this afternoon, then the beach barbecue afterward.

Lane admitted she didn't want to spend the rest of the day alone. She wanted to spend it with Tyler. Changing into warmer clothes for the afternoon, Lane showed up at the field and was welcomed like

an old friend. It touched her that these people were
so open with friendships, and she hated the thought
of any of them learning that she'd been hiding her
true identity. She focused on the field in time to learn
Tyler's number and watch him get tackled by boys
the size of tanks.

Lane winced as Tyler landed with a thud. "That's
going to hurt tomorrow," she said, and beside her,
Laura laughingly agreed.

His family wasn't like hers. Oh, hers was big and
loud and loving sometimes, but the McKays were
actually more friends than siblings. Lane's own
brothers would be in hot competition in a game like
this, trying to steal the show and not play as a team.
She supposed it was because they each felt, in his
own way, that he had to shake the Giovanni name
and be something on his own, something that had
nothing to do with the winery, much to her father's
disappointment. But then, the McKay children
seemed comfortable with their heritage. Go figure.

A few minutes later Tyler was tackled again. He
didn't get up from the ground quite as fast as the last
time. Lane was out of her seat, worried, till he finally
climbed to his feet and limped to the bench. After
another play, the game was over, the alumni suffering a shameful loss to the younger players.

Tyler approached the stands, motioning for Lane
to come to him. She trotted down the bleachers, feeling young and excited. It was silly of course; she
was thirty, after all. But just the same she felt like a
high-school cheerleader with the captain of the football team. Sweaty and covered with black mud, he
smiled down at her, pulling off his helmet.

"I have about five seconds before I collapse in a heap and embarrass myself," he confessed.

She smiled tenderly. "You're hiding it splendidly."

"Good. I'm going to put my arm around you and pretend I'm not leaning on you for support."

She laughed and let him, saying goodbye to his family, then walked with him to the parking lot. She'd walked from her shop, her own car repaired and sitting in the small garage beside her house.

When Tyler stopped beside a big SUV and keyed in the lock code, she frowned. "What happened to the sports car?"

"I traded it in."

The SUV was cherry-red and huge. Lane couldn't imagine driving it without scraping other cars. "Why? I thought you liked the little silver car."

He shrugged. "Outgrew it, I guess." The truth was, since he'd met Lane, Tyler had started looking to the future, and the sports car was impractical. For the first time in three years, he'd considered marriage and a family. And there was a woman he wanted both with.

He frowned as he stripped off the shirt and shoulder pads, then pulled on an old college sweatshirt. When he'd been at the dealership to pick up the repaired car, it seemed right to choose something big enough for a family, not one man who was getting too old to be playing the field. And who didn't want to anymore, anyway. He glanced at Lane. So why wasn't he afraid of getting hurt again?

"Good grief, Tyler, your hand. It looks broken." Gently she grasped his hand, examining the scrapes and swollen finger. "This needs ice right now. Come back to my place."

"Mine's closer and I have to shower and change. Hop in." When she hesitated, a challenge lit his eyes. "Afraid to be alone with me?"

"Of course not. But I'm driving. With that hand, you'll likely crash this car, too." Grinning, he handed her the keys and climbed in the passenger side, giving her directions as she backed out and into traffic. She drove the three blocks to his place, and he groaned like a wounded soldier getting out of the SUV. He still managed to get his cleats off before leading her inside. "Make yourself at home."

She glanced around the sparsely furnished house. It looked as if no one lived here, only visited. She met his gaze. "How about some coffee?" she asked.

"If you can find some—I haven't had the time to shop since the festival started." Tiredly, he mounted the staircase.

"Remember this moment when you want to play ball with teenagers again, McKay," she called to him.

"Your sympathy is touching, darlin'."

"I try." Poor baby, he was moaning with each lift of his foot. She almost offered help, but then turned away and explored his house, liking the design and hating the decor. There was nothing really there to make a statement, and it showed her that Tyler was rarely home and rarely enjoyed it. She put on a small pot of coffee, found mugs and heard the shower running about the time the brewing finished.

A little voice inside her said, *take it to him.* Another said, *Careful. He's up there naked and wet. Near a bed.*

Leaning against the counter, Lane sipped her coffee, debating on whether or not to remain here or go find him. Thoughts of last night in his arms stirred through her mind, calling back images and feelings. The feelings topped the charts, and her breasts tightened inside her lace bra and sent the sensation low in her belly. She admitted she hadn't stood a chance from the moment he'd crashed into her car. She was falling in love with Tyler McKay. The impact of that made her heart ache, suddenly and sharply. She had to tell him the truth.

But she couldn't bring herself to destroy what was growing so strongly between them. Carrying on a silent debate in her mind, she walked through the sparsely decorated house, ending at the foot of the staircase, two cups in her hands and an ice bag tucked under her arm. With a deep breath, she climbed the stairs, listening for the sound of the shower, and was amazed to find four rooms on the second floor. Steam lingered in the air and she followed it, nudging open the bedroom door.

A lavish, four-poster rice bed dominated a room with dark mahogany furnishings and textured fabrics. She imagined them in that grand bed, skin to skin, Tyler hovering over her before he pushed himself inside her. Her insides clamped tight and heat spiraled through her. He was under her skin, tucked in her heart. And when she looked at the open bathroom door, the sound of water and the roll of steam coming toward her, she knew exactly what she was doing. It was time to stop running. From life, from Tyler. Setting the mugs and ice bag aside, she moved to the doorway, watching him.

He had his hands braced on the tile wall, his head down as the spray hit his muscled back, and through the clear glass she studied every glorious inch of him. And there was a lot of him to see. He tipped his head back into the spray and she moved into his line of vision.

He went still, his gaze clashing with hers as the spray beat down on him.

She smiled.

He shut the water off, then reached for the black towel slung over the top of the door. He barely dried his face and chest before wrapping the towel around his waist.

He pushed open the door. "You came up here because you wanted to," Tyler said, fighting an intense need to drag her into his arms. Her being here, now, sent a clear message.

"Yes."

He stepped out. "Do I need to ask you if you're sure?"

"No. You don't." She removed her glasses and tipped her head. "How about you?"

"Oh, darlin'," he growled, taking a step closer. "You have no idea how much I've wanted you here." From the start, he thought. From the moment he first kissed her and felt her holding back, hiding.

Lane kicked off her shoes and toed off her socks. Tyler watched her. His body reacted with amazing swiftness, and when she reached for the hem of her sweater, he gathered her in his arms and kissed her. Hungrily. Wildly. He held her so tightly he brought her off the floor, his hands fisting in her sweater. His mouth crushed hers, and his hands dived under the fabric and palmed warm, smooth skin. He wanted to touch every inch of her, taste her, hear her cry out and tremble in his arms.

He'd never needed anything more than this, with her.

He backed her out of the bathroom, soft carpet and quiet greeting them. He kept kissing her, almost afraid she'd vanish. Then she drew back, crossing her arms and pulling off her sweater. Tyler's gaze raked her as she shimmied out of her slacks and stood still.

He looked his fill as she unpinned her hair. Silky, dark-red hair spilled onto her shoulders, and Tyler wondered how any man could miss this sleeping beauty. She took his breath away, with her narrow waist, and her breasts nearly spilling from the lace bra designed to drive men crazy. And when she leaned back against the bedpost and unfastened the bra, he swallowed. The garment fell, discarded, and Tyler was there, his arms closing around her, his kiss ferocious. The tips of her breasts burned into his skin, and he filled his palm with one soft mound, kneading it gently, loving the sounds she made. That she covered his hand and offered him more.

And he took, lifting her, closing his lips around her tender nipple. She inhaled sharply, bowing in his arms, and Tyler licked, suckled and toyed, and she squirmed in his arms.

"You taste so good."

"It's the body wash," she teased, her hands molding him everywhere she could reach. He chuckled, hooking her knee and pulling her more tightly against him. It wasn't enough. Not till he was inside her. Feeling her body wrap his.

Her touch was silky and strong, and when she reached the towel, she gave it a tug. "I don't think we need this."

Skin met skin, his arousal pressed to her softness, and Tyler felt his control slipping. He stepped back suddenly, shoving his hands through his hair.

"Tyler?"

"Gimme a second. I want you so badly and I want to take my time…"

"There is always later, you know, for the patient side of you."

His gaze flew to hers. She smiled and turned, pressing a knee to his bed. Tyler's throat closed, blood rushing from his head. He got the sexiest view of her behind in a black thong. She reached into the nightstand, flashing him a smile, and grabbed condom packets, then faced him on her knees. She let the condoms rain down over her, then crooked a finger to him.

It took everything in him not to leap on her and shove himself inside her. But he crawled onto the mattress, his weight sinking her toward him. He dragged her between his spread thighs, trapping her, kissing her deeply, trailing his mouth down her throat and bending her back to taste her breasts. Again and again, he nibbled and licked, his hand smoothing down her hip and sliding under the band of her panties.

"We don't need these," he said, and with a sharp twist, he snapped the delicate threads.

Lane laughed, meeting his gaze. "So much for patience."

"It's vastly overrated."

Naked, he pressed her to him, the contact dashing him with heat and untapped energy. She was like a storm and he was about to feel a strike of lightning.

Lane ached, the dull throb she'd experienced when he was near turning to a raging clamor of sights, smells and tastes. She smoothed the hard contours of his chest, and her mouth followed, her tongue slicking over his flat coin nipples. His fingers dug into her hips, his groan like a purring tiger's. The heat of him pressed to her belly, and she closed her fingers around his arousal. In a flash, he captured her wrist. He met her gaze, his eyes hooded with desire.

"I'm already coming apart." He swallowed hard.

"I want to see you shatter," she said, and her fingertips slid heavily over the silken tip of him and down his shaft. He slammed his eyes shut and his breath trembled. She tasted it, sliding her tongue over his lips, then dipping inside. He cracked, devouring her mouth and dragging her onto his lap and spreading her thighs around him and breaking her hold. As much as he was enjoying her touch, he couldn't take much more. He needed to be inside her.

He leaned forward, pushing her onto her back, her hair spilling like cherry wine across his pillows. She smiled up at him, lifting her hips, inviting him to come to her now, and he searched the bed for a condom. She took it from him, rolling it down and didn't let go, opening for him. Braced above her, Tyler trembled as the tip of him pressed to her softness. She was hot and wet, squirming beneath him.

She lifted her hips. "Now, Tyler, please, now."

He entered her with unforgiving slowness, smiling when she begged for more. He pushed deeply, filling her to the hilt and she wrapped her legs around his hips. Braced on his elbows he stared down at her, smoothing her hair back, dropping a kiss on her forehead.

"You're so beautiful."

She smiled. "Flattery will get you anything you want."

"I have what I want right here."

Her eyes misted with tears. "Tyler…"

"My heart's in this, Lane."

"Mine, too, handsome."

He withdrew and plunged, her body closing tightly over his, capturing him, stealing more than his desire. Feminine muscles flexed and clawed, and their tempo increased, a pumping madness that fused them with every stroke.

A match, a perfect fit.

He watched her eyes. He'd seen it once before and it had stolen through his blood, the fire that sparkled, the primal side of her he wanted to unleash.

Lane thought she'd break apart, her heart was pounding so fast. Wanting him all over her, wanting him to explore and taste and stroke and never stop. She felt the connection to him grow and fuse, her body capturing him in a slick glove and taking him deeper into her. She couldn't get enough of him. It was rapture and agony when he left her fully, then plunged home.

Flesh met flesh, muscular and sculpted meshing with soft and yielding. They danced in quick rhythm.

Eyes locked on each other, tingling heat spiraled through her like a tornado, gaining speed and power.

Then it came, the exhilaration only he could give her. The passion she'd waited so long to feel. His arousal throbbed inside her, slick muscle and tender skin quaking with pleasure and sending it streaming through her body.

"Tyler, oh, Tyler."

"I know, baby, I know," he whispered huskily, his gaze locked with hers as his climax roared up his spine like an animal cut loose from a cage. He threw his head back, shuddering, his body flexing against her like a bow strung too tight. Lane gripped his hips, pulling him harder to her, the pulse and throb thrashing them over and over until they never thought it would stop. Then didn't want it to.

The crest shattered him, and tears filled her eyes again, the shocking power of their loving leaving her weak and breathless as the haze faded to a delicate hum in their blood.

Tyler peppered her face and hair with kisses before his mouth settled warmly on hers. He thought his heart might explode, the power of their lovemaking stunning him to the core. When he caught his breath, he rolled to his back taking her with him, pulling her leg over his hip and keeping her close.

Lane gazed into his soft blue eyes and smiled. She loved him. If she'd doubted her heart before, she didn't now. It should make her terrified, but it didn't. It was as if a door tightly locked had been opened in secret. Little by little parts of her poured out and Tyler stole them. Kept them private for her. As much as he pestered and pursued, he was gentle and determined. She wouldn't think of the lies she'd told to protect herself. She'd only think in the here and now. This moment.

"Lane."

"Hmm?"

"You're amazing."

She blushed and kissed him. "I won't tell you what great hip action you have, darling. You'll get conceited." He grinned and toyed with her nipple, then palmed her breast.

"You starting something?" she asked, and he loved the playful look in her eyes.

"I never said I was done."

The phone rang and Tyler glared at it, then reached over and answered.

Lane slid on top of him, folding her arms and watching him.

"Ah, yes, Mom, I'm okay."

Lane covered her mouth to keep from laughing.

"No, it's not broken." He held up his finger, wiggling it. It was still swollen. "No, Lane is with me."

Her eyes flew wide.

"We'll see you tonight on the beach." He hung up.

"I can't believe you told her I was here."

"She can't see us, you know."

Lane started to move away, and Tyler tossed the phone aside and grabbed her, throwing her on her back. "You can't keep hiding, baby."

"I'm not."

"Oh, yeah? Then tell me about your family."

"I did."

His disappointment was written on his face. "Sure. Names and that's it."

"They come with the package, but they aren't me," she said, throwing his own words back at him. "Right now I want you, only you and me."

"Yeah?" His hand slid over the swell of her hip.

"Once is never enough with you, McKay. You're addictive." Straddling his hips, she sat up and wrapped her fingers around him, his eyes flaring as she stroked him. Then she guided him inside her, sinking down onto his hardness till he filled her. She was slick and incredibly hot, and when she thrust her hips against him, Tyler lost all thought, except one. Lane. And that it would take a lifetime to have enough of her.

They'd had to shower and dress, then rush to the beach party before his mother called again.

"Am I wearing a guilty look?"

He frowned down at her, slinging his arm over her shoulders as they made their way down the beach to the bonfire. "No." He kissed the top of her head. "And neither am I. I don't feel the least bit guilty."

"But we're late."

"I needed medical attention." He waved the sprained finger.

"And I needed *your* attention," she said, and he looked at her, a sexy smile twisting his lips. "Which was wonderful."

He tipped his head toward her and whispered, "There's always tonight, darlin'."

Her insides ignited like the fire on the beach, and the thought of waking in his arms was like a treat she'd win if she behaved like a lady in public. Because she didn't want to behave with him in private.

Family and friends greeted the race winners with a loud cheer, and Lane and Tyler were torn apart by people wanting to recap the contest. Over the next couple of hours, they had little time together, but she caught him looking at her when they weren't. She was just as guilty, and when Kate moved up beside her, a baby girl on her hip, Lane turned her attention from the man who'd made love to her this afternoon.

Kate shifted the baby and Lane ached to hold her. When she stroked the child's hair, the baby smiled. Definitely a McKay, Lane thought, and held out her hands. The baby practically leaped into her arms and wrapped her tiny arms around Lane's neck.

Lane rubbed her back, staying near enough to the fire to keep the infant warm.

"You like my brother, don't you," Kate said.

She glanced in Tyler's direction briefly. "Yes, I do." *I love him.*

"I'm glad. It's about time he started dating seriously again."

Lane frowned.

"He didn't tell you about his wedding?" Kate asked.

Lane felt cold dread move up her spine.

"Well, almost wedding. Tyler learned his bride-to-be was marrying him for his money a week before the wedding."

"That's awful."

"Do you want him for his money?"

"I have my own, Kate." She had a trust fund and stocks that would keep her comfortable for a while.

But she admired Tyler's sister for looking out for him. "In fact, I didn't want his attention because he had wealth and power."

Kate blinked. "Okay, that's a first."

"I've seen what it can do to people, the unsavory types it can bring out of the woodwork."

"Butt out, Kate," Tyler said from behind them.

His sister stuck her chin out. "I'm just watching out for you, big brother, and you should have told her."

"What goes on between Lane and me is private."

Kate took her daughter from Lane and faced her older brother. She gazed at him, then smiled softly. "I love you, Ty."

His shoulders sank.

"I'm sorry," Kate went on, "but now that the door is open..." She let the sentence hang and strolled away.

Lane looked at Tyler. "Your ex-fiancée must have hurt you very badly."

"Yes."

"I think I can understand her, though."

"What?"

"She wanted what being married to a McKay would give her, not what being married to *you* would give her." Lane shrugged, shoving her cold hands into her jacket pockets. "She was looking out for herself, her future, and she hurt you in the process." She looked at Tyler and saw anger. "I'm not defending her, believe me," she said quickly. "But if she thought material things were what made her happy and mostly made her feel worthy, then that's where her judgment started. Money and comfort were her highest priority."

Tyler thought about that, and realized she was right. Clarice had been her own worst enemy.

"Did this guy who betrayed you have rotten judgment?" Tyler asked softly.

"Oh, yes, he was out for himself from the start. He said he loved me and that he wanted the same things I did, when it was the farthest thing from the truth. He only wanted what he could get from me."

In her eyes, Tyler saw that the wound was still there. And fear. Was she afraid he'd do the same to her? "And what was that?"

"To hurt my family."

He lifted a brow and was about to ask her to elaborate when she asked, "Did you love her, Tyler?"

"I thought I did. But she was too easy to get over."

"And did you get over her?"

He strolled closer. "I wouldn't have kissed you if I hadn't."

"Ah, a man of honor."

"You're so damn distrusting, you know that?"

"I'm working on that, like my two smiles a day."

Tyler drew her into his arms. "I saw a few of 'em a couple of hours ago." He pushed his fingers into her hair, dislodging the ribbon holding it back. She hurried to redo it, but he grasped her hands, bringing them to his mouth. He kissed her knuckles. "You're so beautiful, Lane. Stop hiding and trust me."

Her gaze searched his. He knew there was more to her past and he deserved to know.

"Tyler…you don't know what you're asking."

"Is it that bad, your past?"

"No, yes…it's hard to explain."

"Don't you know by now that I'm not going to hurt you? That I'm not him?"

She nodded, her throat tight. "I'm not her, either."

"Oh, that I know."

"Just keep remembering that," she said, and held him tightly. "Just keep remembering that."

Ten

Lane felt like Cinderella going to the ball.

Her prince arrived wearing a black tuxedo and escorted her to his coach, a sleek black limousine waiting at the curb. The night was crisp and dark, the moon high in the winter sky. Twinkling lights still wrapped the lampposts and laced the trees, brightening the night like stars trickling down from a midnight heaven. A glorious night for a ball, she thought as they neared the limousine. The driver opened the door, gawking at her as she ducked inside.

Tyler noticed and sent the young man an annoyed look.

The chauffeur murmured, ''Hey, I'm a guy. It's hard not to look, sir.''

Tyler climbed in beside her and realized as they rode the distance to the country club that he was possessive. Not something he was used to, but he realized he was enjoying the new feeling. He took Lane's hand and immediately she laced her fingers with his.

"Thank you, Tyler. It's been a while since I've been out like this."

He only smiled, his gaze moving over the dark-green hooded cloak she wore. That she'd concealed her gown from him piqued his curiosity. She's changed, he thought. Before his eyes, she'd shed the dowdy appearance she'd used to keep him and everyone else back. He'd been with her almost every night since the sailboat race, and waking with her in his arms left him content and at the same time scared as hell. The thought of *not* having her with him had outweighed the barriers he'd erected. He admitted that they'd crumbled pretty easily the minute he saw her, anyway, and he'd decided he was ready to give up not trusting women. Especially when he found a woman that trust came so hard for.

The limo drew to a halt, and Tyler slid out, turning back to offer his hand to Lane. He caught a glimpse of long, stockinged legs as she slid gracefully from the car. He wrapped an arm around her waist, holding her close, and her gloved hands rested on his shoulders.

"Remember me sometime tonight."

"Oh, Tyler, I could never forget you." She stroked his cheek with a gloved finger.

"You say that now, but my friends can be pretty persuasive."

She rose up on her toes, kissing him. "So can you."

Smiling, he escorted her inside. The gathering was alive with color, and dancers were already filling the floor. A band played softly from the stage, and elegantly decorated tables rimmed the ballroom. Christmas was hinted at in the boughs of greenery, and the history of the town showed in liveried waiters serving champagne and canapés. It was beautiful and she smiled.

"Lane? Your cloak."

She looked at him, then loosened the braided frog before pushing back the hood. Velvet pooled on her shoulders briefly before he pulled it from her shoulders. Her hair cascaded down her back in a long tumble of auburn curls.

"Wow." His gaze roamed the deep-green beaded gown that fit her like a second skin. His heart did a quick hop, and pride spread through him. She was definitely one of a kind.

She smiled, blushing, something she did a lot around him. "I'm glad you like it."

"And I'd like to get you out of it right now."

She leaned into him, her hand on his chest. "Can you wait a few hours?" she whispered for his ears alone. "Because I'd rather be alone with you than with people staring at me."

"Then you shouldn't be so pretty."

She laughed lightly. "Boy, are you laying it on."

He scoffed, then nodded past her. "Look."

She turned and faced the crowd, and Lane's first thought was, *I shouldn't have come back full blast.* She should have eased into this, let people get used to seeing the dowdy Miss Douglas changing bit by bit before they met Elaina Honora Giovanni. Earlier this evening she'd sifted through her closet, the need to keep a low profile, gown-wise, warring with the strong desire to shed her self-imposed restrictions and be who she really was. This evening meant a lot to her, and it meant more to Tyler. These were his friends and colleagues, people from his town, and she wouldn't dare arrive in anything but her very best. Yet now, people were staring, and she felt as if she'd just opened Pandora's Box. All she'd worked for could turn to dust.

"Oh, no."

"Oh, yes. Come on, there's Kyle. Poor guy, he's dateless."

The minute they reached their table, people swarmed them. And before some other man could take her from him, Tyler pulled her out onto the dance floor.

"Oh, Tyler, I'm sorry."

"Why? Don't you think I like being with the most attractive, sought-after woman at the ball?"

"But I know you do a lot of business here."

"Not tonight."

"Well, you'd think I'd done some transformation like the frog prince or something." She still didn't like the attention.

"Lane, honey, the gown alone is a transformation."

Okay, maybe the gown was a bit over the top. She'd chosen it because it hadn't been seen by the public, had never made it to the showing because the stories Dan Jacobs had printed had generated paparazzi and cruel jokes. And destroyed her reputation and career. But covering her now was her best work, nearly sheer, dark-green silk dripping with beads. It gave the fabric weight and folds where it dipped low enough in the front to offer an enticing glimpse of cleavage. The sleeves were velvet, beaded and clinging to her arms past her wrists, giving the gown a period flare, but it was the dangerously bare back, revealing the curve of her spine, and the sweeping fishtail hem that set the gown apart. Almost femme fatale in its mystery. Though the body-hugging fit didn't hide much.

"Ignore the stares," he whispered, seeing her discomfort and wanting to ease it. "I must say, though, I never thought I'd know a woman who didn't want the attention of a few dozen men."

"I want the attention of one man, and right now, I have it. Call me lucky."

Me, too, he thought, sweeping her across the dance floor. She moved with regal grace and elegance, and he forgot about the people staring, the whispers of his past, their surprise at the new Lane Douglas. Possession and something he wasn't ready to name rose in him, and he pulled her closer. Like a kid allowed up late on Christmas Eve, he didn't want this night to end.

Neither did Lane, and after a few minutes, she forgot about everyone else there. She saw only Tyler, recognizing why she loved him so much and how easily she could lose it. The risks were high, but it was unfair to keep secrets from him any longer. She'd tell him tonight and take her chances. The biggest one in her life.

As the evening wore on, it almost hurt to look at him. Tyler surprised her by rarely leaving her side,

and if she didn't know better, she'd swear he was
staking his claim. Good. Because she was, too, and
when she danced with anyone else, her gaze always
sought him. The press were let in at nine and Lane
avoided the cameras, and Nalla, bless her, kept stepping in front of a shot for her. She was wearing one
of Lane's designs again, and in a midnight-blue, vel-
vet-and-silk affair dusted with crystals, she looked
like an elfin queen.

Lane and Tyler shared one last dance before the
evening drew to a close, both wanting to be away in
private. They slid into the limousine, and Lane
leaned into him, resting her head on his shoulder. He
wrapped his arm around her and kissed the top of
her head. "Thank you," he whispered. "I'd never
had a good time at those society functions till tonight."

"I liked it. It kind of gears you up for Christmas."
Her hand smoothed his shirtfront. He looked smash-
ing in the tuxedo, as if he was born to it, and the
desire she'd capped all night blossomed. She slid her
hand to his thigh, teasing him, moving slowly upward and molding him. He hardened beneath the
black fabric and bent his head to kiss her, the contact
moist and heated.

Her hands grew bolder, demanding, and his slid
inside her cloak, shaping her spine and dipping under
the beaded silk.

He blinked. "You're naked beneath that dress."

She smiled. "Panties ruin the line."

He groaned. "If I'd known that, we'd have left
hours ago."

"It wouldn't have been proper."

''Yeah, but me walking around with this—'' he pushed her hand against his arousal ''—wouldn't have been, either.''

She laughed softly and when the driver pulled to a stop at his house, they were out of the car and racing up the walk like children. Tyler kissed her and kissed her, fumbling with the keys, yet refusing to let her go. She took them, opened the door and yanked him inside. In seconds he had her against the wall, cloak fallen to the floor, his jacket joining it and they battled for tastes of each other as Lane loosened his tie, then plucked at the shirt studs. They pinged to the floor and he buried his face in her breasts.

''I want you,'' he muttered.

''Take me.'' She sank her fingers into his hair, her body trembling with want.

''I don't think I'm gonna—''

''Don't think, Tyler. I'm not. I'm only feeling and I want you now.'' She pushed him back and reached behind her neck, pulling the single transparent string that kept the dress on. She wiggled and the gown slithered down her body to pool at her ankles. She stood in his foyer, naked except for stockings and heels.

Tyler didn't think he'd ever seen anything sexier, but then she picked up the dress and, proud as you please, mounted the stairs to the second floor, the gown snaking over the steps behind her. On the landing, she twisted and looked back.

''Are you coming?''

He swallowed. ''Woman, you have a wild side I'm just discovering.''

He raced up the staircase, taking them two at a time, and found her in his bedroom, lounging in a chair. She looked like a centerfold, and he walked across the room, stripping off his shirt.

She couldn't wait and pulled him down. Tyler fell to his knees, his hips spreading her thighs as he ravished her mouth, his hands combing her breasts, kneading the firm mounds. He broke the kiss to wrap his lips around a hardened pink nipple. He suckled hard and she gasped, holding him there. Fire pulsed through her, spreading under her skin. No other man, she thought, no other made her feel this cherished.

She tipped her head back, offering herself, telling him how good he made her feel. Need clawed. Heat and passion raced to join and dance, and Lane twisted in the chair, panting, her hands scraping over his chest, his shoulders, then seeking the belt of his trousers. She needed to feel his skin, his strength.

The simple touch, a flutter of her fingertips over his arousal, inflamed him. But Tyler wanted to taste and savor, wanted to watch her break apart with the pleasure he gave her, and he pushed her back into the chair, kissing her taut belly, dragging his tongue over the bend of her naked hip. Like a wild stag he scented her, nipping her soft flesh, then hooked one of her knees over the arm of the chair. She met his gaze, searing him with a sultry look before he lifted the other leg, spreading her. Then he touched her and she arched off the chair, her breath hissing. She met his gaze again as he pushed two fingers inside her.

"Oh, Tyler."

He thrust and withdrew. "I want to hear you scream."

"I want you inside me. Now." She reached for him, gasping for her next breath, her nerves careening with pleasure. But he shook his head, a devilish smile on his lips as he scooped his hands under her buttocks. Lane was helpless as he lifted her to his mouth and covered her. She shrieked as he drove his tongue into her soft folds. She flexed wildly and he held her tighter, pushing her legs onto his shoulders. He was unrelenting as he sent her to the peak like a rocket to the sky. She pushed and squirmed against him, and her muscles quivered, but he spread her wider still, his tongue circling the bead of her sex.

She fractured, calling his name, and he pushed two fingers inside her. She begged him to join her now, to share this with her. Tyler lowered her to the chair, opened his trousers, and pushed into her.

Her climax trapped him. Squeezing hard. He withdrew and plunged deeply. She wrapped her legs around his waist, and he pulled her from the chair onto the floor, mashing her to him, pushing, pushing.

They were primal, savage in their need for each other. Heat and passion boiled to heights neither had expected. Tyler laid her on her back, shoving into her, and she answered, her strong legs slamming him back to her.

Gazes locked, bodies pumping wildly, the power of it pushing them across the floor. Her breath caught with his, and he watched ecstasy erupt in her eyes, felt it rip through her body and spill into him. She took him with her, and rapturous sensations tore through him, leaving only pleasure behind.

"Oh, my love," she moaned, and Tyler felt his heart break open. She had tears in her eyes, her fingers dribbling over his face, pushing into his hair before she kissed him hungrily. "I love you, Tyler," she said, sobbing a little. His gaze raked her beautiful face. "I didn't want to, but I do."

He looked down at her, scraping her hair back off her face. "Lane, darlin', I…" Tyler wasn't sure what he was about to say, for the words locked in his throat. Couched in old fears.

She only smiled a little sadly, hushing anything he was about to say and not mean, and holding him tightly. Tyler squeezed her, locking her more tightly to him, and Lane wondered if she'd ever have a man return her love and mean it. She told herself to be satisfied with this time with Tyler. That one word, one call could ruin everything for her, and she feared that time was running out.

After a few moments, he stood and carried her to his bed, laying her in the center. He stepped back, holding her gaze, a strange wariness in his eyes as he stripped, them climbed into bed beside her. She didn't hesitate and opened her arms to him. They sank into an erotic world of love and passion, sharing each other through the night and blocking out the world.

Lane stirred in his bed, reaching for him and finding the space beside her empty. "Tyler?"

"I'm in here," he called from the bathroom.

Lane curled on her side, pulling his pillow close and burying her face in his scent. Her heart ached and she wondered at the wisdom of telling him she loved him when he didn't love her back. Ribbons of doubt fluttered through her. She knew he cared deeply for her, but he'd made no promises, no declarations, and so she needed to be satisfied with the moments they had now. Still, her heart ached for more with him, for a life and future. And she knew she had to tell him the truth. Now. Her heart started pounding and she slipped from the bed, looking for something to cover herself with and spying his robe on the chair. Clothing was a necessary barrier when talking to Tyler, she thought. And no touching. He made it impossible for her to keep a thought in her head when he touched her.

The phone rang and she was about to reach for it, then hesitated.

"Let the machine pick it up," he said from the bath. "I don't want to ruin your reputation."

She smiled and slipped on the too-big robe as the message played. Then a voice came on.

"*Buon giorno,* Elaina."

Lane paled, her heart dropping to her stomach. *Dan Jacobs.* She snatched up the phone. "You have the wrong number." How did he find her here, she wondered, looking toward the window and imagining him calling from nearby on a cell phone.

"Not a chance. I'd recognize that voice anywhere."

"You're mistaken."

"Oh, yeah? Well, I've got pictures to prove I'm right."

"What!" Pictures? When? Where?

"I didn't know you could dance so well, Elaina, and the race, that was something. It was on the Associated Press because it was a fluff piece, small-town record broken. It'll hit the networks if I let it."

"No. Oh, God, Dan, don't do this."

"You owe me a story." His voice was mean and dark.

"You've already written enough. There is nothing more to tell." Lane glanced around, hearing the shower running. Her heart was pounding so fast she thought she'd faint. "I don't owe you anything!"

"If you don't talk to me, these pictures will be leaked in an hour. You look cute in navy blue."

The race, she thought, and tried not to cry. "Don't, please don't. I'm begging you. Don't destroy my life again."

For a second, Dan was quiet on the other end of the line. "He doesn't know who you are, does he?"

Lane slammed the phone down, then erased Dan's voice from the machine. Hot tears burned her eyes. Too late. It was too late. She'd lose everything. Falling in love with Tyler was going to come with a high price. She didn't give a damn about the press anymore, only what it would do to Tyler and his family. The smear, the implications. He'd be as ruined as she had been. Dan Jacobs could hound her, but not Tyler.

Oh, God, she loved him so much, and it was shattering before they had a chance. She looked toward the bathroom, then searched for her clothing. She had to stop Dan Jacobs. She didn't know how, but she couldn't let this hurt Tyler. Oh, Lord, she couldn't. Not now.

Tyler came out of the bathroom, belting a terrycloth robe in time to see Lane grab up her gown. "Lane, baby, where are you going?"

"I have to leave."

Tyler frowned. "Wait a second."

"No, I have to leave now." She couldn't look at him.

Tyler crossed to her, grabbing her arms. "You're crying. My God, tell me what's wrong."

"I can't, I can't." She was sobbing openly now and knew she was in a corner.

Tyler pulled her into his arms, and she let out a long, shaky breath, wilting against him. "Who was on the phone?" he asked.

Say it, a voice demanded. *Say it now.* "Dan Jacobs. A reporter."

"What did he say to you?"

"Nothing I haven't been dreading for the past two years."

Tyler's frown deepened. "Tell me, baby."

Lane pushed out of his arms and wrapped his robe more tightly around herself. She stared at him, feeling as if the floor was opening and she was about to tumble into darkness. But she had to tell him, and she met his gaze. "Dan was the man who betrayed me. A reporter, only he didn't tell me that. He claimed he was a photographer, even had a portfolio." She made a bitter sound, feeling more foolish than she had the day she learned who Dan really was. "He dated me, seduced me and said he loved me— just to get a story."

"On what? Selling books?"

She lifted her chin a bit and stared at the man she loved and would lose. "On me. My name is not Lane Douglas."

Tyler felt his blood drain from his face. His chest tightened painfully.

"Douglas was my grandmother's name, and Lane is short for…for Elaina."

His fingers closed into fists at his sides. "Elaina who?" he asked carefully.

"Giovanni."

His gaze moved over her body in his robe, then her face, her long sleep-tumbled hair. Everything slipped into place and the picture became painfully clear. Her near reclusiveness, avoiding talking about herself. The way she'd looked in that gown. Like a starlet. The familiarity he'd felt a couple of times last night. He'd seen her in the papers, on TV. And now some guy wanted an interview? "Giovanni, as in the largest winery in the world? Those Giovannis?"

"Yes."

Good God. "You lied to me." His voice was dead when he said it. She'd let him love her and deceived him.

"I was protecting myself."

"From what?"

She flinched at his angry tone. "That jerk destroyed my life. I was a designer—"

"I know exactly who and what you were," he interrupted, leveling her a look she never wanted to see. "I know all about the family, the mob connections—"

"There aren't any! No one will believe me."

He scoffed, too hurt to think about that. "I don't give a damn about a reporter or your family, *Elaina*. You *lied* to me. After all we've shared, you still lied. You should have been an actress, because I fell for your act like a fool."

"Tyler, no!"

He stepped right over her words. "When I was making love to you, you didn't think you should tell me who you really were?"

She winced, the hurt in his voice slicing through her heart, and for a second stopped its beating. "I couldn't then, because it was too late, I'd let it go too far."

"Why couldn't you trust me with the truth?"

"I'm telling you now and look how you're reacting!"

He glared at her, disgusted, all the feelings that Clarice had left behind rising to the surface. "You aren't even the woman I knew."

Her posture stiffened. "Yes, I am. I might not have been paying attention to my appearance, but I'm the same person." *The woman who loves you.* "I didn't tell anyone because I've tried for two years to forget. You don't know what it's like to have your face printed in the morning paper, your most intimate thoughts shared with the world. I couldn't even buy groceries without someone following me and snapping a picture. That's what Dan Jacobs did. He took my love and used it for a lead story!"

A small wave of sympathy moved through him, but Tyler could only feel his heart folding in on itself. And in that one moment, while he was bleeding inside, he realized he loved her. Truly loved her. Which only made him hurt more.

"Damn you, Lane. I could have helped you. I would have protected you!"

"It would have ruined your reputation. Maybe even your company. The press is still screaming mafia connections, Dan is still hounding my whole family. I couldn't bring you into this. I tried to stay away from you, you know that,'' she defended. ''I didn't want this to backfire on you.''

''I can take care of myself.''

''Yeah, well, I thought I could take care of myself, too. Within a couple of weeks, my career turned into a joke, I lost a major department store deal and lost my company. My life became a fishbowl.'' She reached for her clothing, wondering how she was going to get home in an evening gown without bringing attention to herself. Then she didn't care.

Tyler watched her shimmy into the gown, remembering her doing the opposite last night. ''Wait. I'll take you home,'' he said.

''No, thank you.'' She secured the tie under her hair and looked at him. ''I've managed alone just fine.'' Her voice cracked. ''I can do it again.'' She grabbed his car keys and headed out the door. ''Goodbye, Tyler.''

Tyler couldn't move. He wanted to go after her, but her lies kept him rooted to the floor. *Stop her,* a voice in his head screamed. But she'd lied about everything in her life. And a wounded part of him said she'd lied about her love for him, too.

Eleven

It didn't take long for Tyler to get a taste of what Lane, or rather, Elaina, had experienced before coming to Bradford.

And it was ugly.

A band of newspeople had made camp across the street from his house, for crying out loud. One idiot had tried to climb the live oak in his yard for a picture into his bedroom and ended up in the azalea bushes. He'd managed to ignore them for two days, but now they were like dogs after a bone.

"Did you know who she was, Mr. McKay?" a reporter shouted as Tyler walked to his office.

"Were you aware of the Giovanni family's mob connections?" said another.

"Were you hiding her, McKay?"

"Just how intimate were you with Miss Giovanni?"

That got him. Tyler rounded on the group that had followed him to the door of his office building, and a few backstepped. The way he was feeling, he would enjoy punching a few faces and not mind the jail time he got for it. Anything was better than the emptiness. He'd never felt so miserable.

"Get off my property before I have you all arrested for trespassing."

"It's a free country, McKay."

"You're right, but I own this land." He turned to the doors, stepping inside. The little group of reporters rushed toward the building. He locked the doors and looked at the guard and the receptionist. "Call DJ and tell him what's going on," he said, referring to the sheriff. "I want those idiots off McKay property."

"Yes, sir," the receptionist said, picking up the phone. "If we're getting this—" she gestured at the people gathered outside the door "—then what is Miss Douglas, I mean, Ms. Giovanni, suffering?"

Tyler's features tightened. He knew. His mother had taken pleasure in raking him over the coals and informing him that Lane hadn't left her house because of the press. Her customers couldn't get into her shop, and she couldn't get out of her house. And worse, Lane didn't seem to care.

He strode to his office and slammed the door shut behind him, tempted to throw his briefcase at the plate-glass window and watch it shatter. The thought of never seeing her again, touching her, was driving him insane. He wondered what she was thinking and feeling. He wanted to be near her. Wanted her to turn to him. But why should she? She had and he'd turned

his back on her, he realized. He didn't have to ask
if Lane regretted telling him she loved him. He'd
recognized it in the look on her face when he'd let
her walk out.

He'd broken her heart.

And it was killing him inside.

He stared at the phone, then grabbed the handset
and punched in her number. He got her answering
machine and imagined her sitting there, staring at the
phone. Alone. Hanging up without saying anything,
he dropped into his leather chair and spun it toward
the window.

Lane's face flashed in his mind, the absolute des-
olation she wore when she'd walked out of his house.
As if she'd expected him to turn on her. And he had.
His heart ached more than he'd ever imagined possible. Damn, he thought, rubbing his face with both
hands. This stinks.

She wasn't a dowdy bookseller. She was an heiress, for heaven's sake. A famous fashion designer.
No wonder she could make those costumes so
quickly, and that gown. And despite his hurt, his
body tightened as he remembered how every man at
the ball had wanted her. And the pride he'd felt because she was his. His woman. His love.

And he'd lost her. He'd turned his back on her and
lost her.

Seeing how the tabloid press chased him, he didn't
have trouble imagining how it had been for her. He'd
read the articles and headlines on the Internet, and
each one was like a knife that hacked at his con-
science.

He stared blankly out the window and wondered

which was worse—a man who was left with only his pride or a man who left the woman he loved to the wolves.

A second later he was out of the chair and heading to the door.

Lane had been on her latest crying jag when the phone rang. She listened, waiting for the caller to speak, knowing it had to be another reporter, because Tyler hadn't spoken to her in two days. He hadn't called. But when she heard her brother's voice, she snatched up the phone.

"Angel, I could just kill you."

"I'm sorry, kitten. I didn't mean for this to happen."

"Yeah, I've heard that before. Your life has ruined mine!" She swallowed, fighting tears and wishing Tyler was here to lean on. "How did you get this number?"

"Papa gave it to me."

"The traitor."

"I begged, because there's something I need to tell you. Can you meet with me?"

"Like I can get out the door without someone attacking me."

"Try. We have to talk."

He sounded troubled. "Where?"

"There's a little diner near the turnoff to a place called Hardeeville."

"I know where it is. This is my town, remember."

"An hour."

A few minutes later, Lane braved the crush of reporters and made it to her car. A half hour later she

walked into the diner. Her brother rose from a booth
in the back, looking as handsome as ever. He wore
jeans and a leather bomber jacket like Tyler's, not
his normal uptown look. Angel had never stepped
out the door wearing anything less than his eye-
catching best. On top of that, he hadn't shaved and
his hair was nearly brushing his shoulders. As she
stopped in front of him, she couldn't decide if she
wanted to hug him or hit him.

"Hi, kitten."

Lane folded, letting him hold her for a long moment before they parted and slid into the booth.
"Talk, brother," she said in Italian.

He glanced around and leaned forward. "I've been
working with the authorities for three years now."
He, too, spoke in Italian.

"Authorities? You mean the FBI?"

"Yeah, sorta."

Lane listened as Angel told her that the FBI approached him for his help, and used his high profile
status to make friends with suspected mafias and
learn all he could.

"Oh, my God." She fell back into the cracked
leather seat. No wonder he wouldn't say anything
and had kept to himself. Infiltrating the mob? Part of
her was intensely proud of the bravery that took, and
another part was still smarting that she'd paid the
price for it. "Damn you, Angel. Your jaunt as a spy
ruined me. Because you said nothing to clear this up,
I lost everything, including the man I loved."

He scowled. "Dan Jacobs is a bug."

"Not him, you idiot. Good intentions or not, you
should have warned me and the family. Jacobs might

have used me for a story, but you used all of us. It was cruel and unfair, Angel. I had to lie to people I care about and I lost the man I love because of it.''

''You're in love?'' He smiled. ''That's great. What's his name?''

Ever the romantic, she thought. ''It doesn't matter anymore.'' She was too tender to talk about Tyler to her brother.

''I guess this means you won't forgive me.''

She sent him a hard look. ''Give me one reason any of us should.''

''We got the bad guys and I'm training with the FBI.''

She blinked. ''Are they nuts?''

''Surprisingly, I'm good at their sort of work.'' He released a sigh and picked up a paper napkin. For several moments, he watched his moves as he molded it into the shape of a mushroom. ''We were born into money, Elaina, and I never worked hard like you or Sophia or Ricco, for something of my own. I won't get into what happened to make me aware of my shortcomings, but I didn't like who I saw in the mirror, and I didn't deserve all that money.''

Whatever happened had changed him drastically. ''And now you do?''

Only his gaze shifted and Lane saw a dangerous side of her brother she never thought existed. ''I doubt I ever will, but at least it's being put to good use. It gave my life meaning.''

''I'm glad you've found a true purpose, but it destroyed my career in the process.''

He scowled at her bitterness. ''You could get it all

back and you know it. You chose to fold up shop."
At her glare, he put up his hand. "Okay, okay. I'm
not shifting blame, but are you ever going to forgive
me?"

"I'll make the effort." Because he seemed to need
it so badly, enough to risk coming to her. Her lips
curved into a soft smile. "I'm proud of you, Angel."

He melted into the leather seat with relief.
"Thanks, sis. So who's this man you love?"

Her expression closed and she stood up to leave.

He leaped after her, grasping her hand. "I'm sorry,
Elaina. If I could make things right for you, I
would."

"You can't, Angel. There is only one person who
can make it right." She cleared her throat. "And he
doesn't want me anymore."

Tyler pushed his way through the throng of reporters on his way to A Novel Idea, but couldn't get
more than five steps from the curb. They shouted the
same questions as they had before, and Tyler ignored
them until one man said, "Tell us, Mr. McKay, is
Elaina a tiger in bed?"

Tyler froze, then turned slowly. A blond man
smirked and pushed a microphone in his face. Tyler's
gaze dropped to the man's press tag. And without a
thought, he drew his arm back and landed a hard
punch to Dan Jacobs's jaw. The man's eyes rolled
back and he fell to the ground. Cameras flashed, but
Tyler didn't care.

He pointed at Jacobs. "That's for Elaina." He
looked at the paparazzi and said, "Why don't you

ask Jacobs here how he lied, cheated and betrayed Elaina Giovanni for a story that was never there?''

Reporters then swarmed Jacobs, still struggling to get to his feet. Tyler walked to the door and pounded on it. "Elaina!" When she didn't open the door, he stepped out on the lawn, ready to make a fool of himself. "Elaina!" he shouted, and the upper-floor window opened.

Lane stuck her head out. "Go away, Tyler. Please.''

She's been crying, he thought, and ached for her. "I'm not going anywhere. You either let me in or I'm going to stay right here and say what I have to say to the world.''

Lane looked at the reporters, at Dan Jacobs clutching his jaw. "All right.''

Tyler went to the back of the house and waited till she opened the door. He paused only long enough to deliver a dark glare at the people who'd followed him up the steps.

Inside she locked the door and headed upstairs without so much as looking at him. "Welcome to my world.''

Tyler climbed the curved staircase, pulling out his cell phone and dialing. "DJ, what are you doing to get these idiots off Lane's property?" When he reached the landing, he saw that she had perched on the window seat in her living room. "Not good enough," he said to the sheriff. "Her customers can't get in and she can't get out. I call that interference with free trade.'' He listened to DJ for a moment, then said, "We're allowing this to happen to one of our own. And I don't care if they're across the street or in the river. Just get them back.'' He shut off the phone, pocketing it.

''Thank you,'' Lane said. ''The police never helped me before, and I saw no reason to ask them now.''

He crossed to the window seat, pushing back the curtain to see the horde on the lawn, drinking coffee while waiting, some accosting passersby, who ignored them and moved on. ''This is madness.''

''Yes, well, at least they haven't printed pictures of us.'' Her voice wavered and Tyler felt it claw him down to his heels. ''You won't have to worry.''

''You think I give a damn about those people and what they think?''

''It doesn't really matter now, does it? I didn't want this to backfire on you, and it has. But I did what I had to do to survive and don't have any regrets except how we ended.''

Panic slithered through him. ''We aren't done, baby.''

She looked away. ''It won't stop. My brother can't come forward—he's working with the FBI. There'll be no end to this.'' She gestured to the window, then turned to face him. ''I have to leave.''

''No! It's running again, Elaina.''

Hearing him call her by her real name drove an agonizing wedge into her. She'd wanted that for so long and hated that it gave her such pleasure when she knew he didn't love her.

''It's survival, Tyler. I lied to survive. I could not trust you with the truth and when I did, you turned on me.''

''I know. I'm sorry, baby. But I couldn't believe

you'd lie about who you were. That you couldn't trust me.''

''Oh, Tyler, I did, but I didn't want to risk ruining what we had.''

''Still have,'' he said intensely, sitting beside her, and when she tried to move away, he caught her hands, gripping them tightly. ''Look at me, baby.''

Lane lifted her gaze and Tyler folded inside. Such hopelessness, he thought.

''Why are you here? What do you want from me?''

''I want you to forgive me.''

Her brows shot up.

''I couldn't see what you'd given up for a little peace and quiet until those vultures showed up. My God, Elaina, you gave up everything to be left alone.''

Her shoulders shifted. ''It's one thing living in the public eye, and another when they know what you wear to bed. But I can't change who I am. I tried and failed.''

''I don't want you to change. The thought of not being with you has scared me for weeks now.''

''Why?''

''Because I know you wanted to be with me for who I am as a man, not for the McKay name and all its trappings. It never mattered to you what I had, but who I was. That was so foreign to me. And it had never mattered who you were, either. Lane or Elaina, you are still the same person.''

''But you let me leave, Tyler.''

''I know, baby, and I'm ashamed of it. I should have fought your battle with you. I'm sorry.'' She was quiet and he tried to look under her bent head. "Am I forgiven?"

She met his gaze again. "Yes."

"I can't give you a life without notoriety, Elaina. My company, my family, we draw attention."

Her heart did a funny little skip. "Privacy has its drawbacks. I don't think I realized how lonely I was till I met you and your family."

"Me, neither." He frowned. "I had family and friends, but I was as alone as you were."

"What do you mean?"

He drew a deep breath. "I was alone till I fell in love with you."

She shot off the seat and moved away, choking on her tears. "Tyler, please don't say it if you don't mean it. I couldn't take it."

He came to her, forcing her around and tipping her chin up. "Listen to me, Elaina Honora Giovanni. I look at you and know that I've never been in love before." When she opened her mouth to remind him of his past, he hushed her. "No, never. Because I'm dying without you. And I'll never survive if you don't love me back." Her eyes teared rapidly. "And I'm sorry I had to break your heart to realize it."

"Tyler."

"I love you, Elaina. I love you so much it's killing me to not be with you."

"Oh, Tyler. I love you, too!" she cried, and he slid his arms around her, gently pulling her close. He buried his face in the bend of her throat, inhaling the scent he'd missed like breathing. He leaned back, his mouth brushing hers, and the heat between them ignited.

"I never could resist you," he said. "Never."

He smiled, cupping her face in his broad palms and kissing her hard, then meeting her gaze. For a long moment he simply stared, and Tyler saw their future in her eyes—wild, passionate and fun.

"I've been miserable without you," he said. "The past two days have been pure hell, and I never want to go through that again."

"Nor do I."

"Then will you marry me?"

She blinked, stunned. He dipped into his pocket as he took her hand. "Marry me, Elaina. Come live in that big house with me and make it a home. Make babies with me." He swallowed, his emotions crowding in on him. "Let me spend the rest of my life showing you how much I love you."

Lane looked at the ring he held poised at the end of her finger. "Tyler."

He waited as she stared at the ring. At last she lifted her gaze to his. "Yes." Her smile brightened his heart. "Yes!"

He slid the ring onto her finger, then slipped his arms around her and kissed her hungrily. He showered her face with kisses, then picked her up, laughing as he spun her around. Lane felt light, the burdens she carried for so long lifting with his love.

Shouts from outside colored the air, and for a long moment they ignored them. Lane wanted Tyler naked in her bed to do some more making up, but he had other plans.

He let her go and headed to the door. "Tyler, don't! Talking to them will just make it worse."

"Not this time."

Tyler was downstairs opening the front door to her shop when Lane caught up with him. Reporters rushed the officers trying to keep them back on the other side of the street, and bulbs flashed.

Tyler just stood still and when his mother, sister, brother-in-law and brother pushed their way through the crowd, he smiled and drew Lane close. She was nearly in tears.

His mother glared at the reporters. "I can see no one ever taught you people good manners," she delivered with pure Southern sting. "You don't come to a house till you're invited. Now get off this porch." The intruders stepped back to the sidewalk.

Tyler stared at the reporters till they fell quiet, then said, "I'm Tyler McKay, and I'm in love with Elaina Giovanni."

Lane beamed at him. His mother gave a delighted shriek and his sister squeezed Lane's hand. He ignored the questions of her fake identity and continued. "I've asked her to marry me and—" he looked down at her "—she's accepted."

"Miss Giovanni? If this true?"

"Yes, it most definitely is. I love him."

Laura, Kyle, Kate and Tyler surrounded her, and she knew she'd never felt so loved and protected in her life.

"She's a McKay now," Kyle said. "So if you mess with her—"

The matriarch interjected, "Y'all mess with all of us."

Lane laughed, hugging Tyler. Her world had been so dark and dismal before he came into it, and with his smile and Southern charm, he'd awakened her, made her see that hiding wasn't the solution and that facing problems head on, together, was the way to go.

As rapid-fire questions peppered the air, Tyler stroked her hair back and tipped up her chin, giving her a light kiss he knew would be on the front page of a tabloid in the morning. He didn't care. He wanted everyone to know that he loved her, that he'd protect her from anyone who'd try to destroy their happiness.

"I love you," she whispered, and he knew he'd never get tired of hearing the words. Despite his wealth and power, no other moment compared to this. He felt humbled by the woman in his arms. A woman who'd given up her lifestyle for a little peace in a small Southern town.

And without realizing it, it was *she* who had rescued *him.*

She'd enchanted him from the first moment, and for a second or two, he felt like a prince, the one who, with a single kiss, woke Sleeping Beauty from her slumber, to be rewarded with her love and the chance of a real happily-ever-after.

Epilogue

Christmas Eve, two years later

Noise and music filled the cinnamon-scented air. His house was busting at the seams. There were so many McKays and Giovannis, it was hard to tell whose children were whose. Tyler searched for his wife, then gave up and leaned against the door frame.

The words eat, drink, and be merry didn't come close with these people, and here he'd thought McKays were loud. But Giovannis talked at the top of their lungs, and their hand gestures had sent more than one person diving to save a figurine or a lamp. But he liked them, had enjoyed their company off and on ever since he and Elaina had married in a wedding carried by the press and television news.

But that, thank God, had been the end of it. The

FBI had cleared her family of any suspicion, and the press faded away. Life was oddly normal and happy, he thought, smiling as Elaina's mother, Lionetta, gave a gift to his mother.

"Hey there."

He twisted, watching Elaina come down the stairs, her body wrapped in floor-length burgundy velvet and showing off her round belly. Tyler didn't think he'd ever seen anything more beautiful and graceful than his wife carrying their child.

He held out his arm to her, and she cuddled close and sighed. "Tired?" He pressed his lips to the top of her head.

"A little." Elaina gazed out over the crowd. Her mother, for once looking like a normal mom, was sitting on her father's lap. This was the love Elaina remembered. The prospect of being a Nana must have changed her.

Tyler looked down at Elaina, noticing the strained look on her face. "You sure you're okay?"

"Uh-huh." Then she flinched and added, "but it's not something a doctor and a sterile environment wouldn't help."

Tyler nodded, then her words sank in. "Oh, man." His eyes widened as she clutched her belly. "You've been hiding this all day, haven't you?"

"I didn't want to spoil the dinner. You know how much food Nalla and your mother cooked."

"Forget the dinner." He scooped her up in his arms and for a second didn't know where to go. She tapped him and pointed to the sofa.

Everyone fell silent as he laid her gently on the

cushions, then the noise rose to deafening proportions. It was Kate who cut through the din.

"Kyle, get the car and bring it around. David," she said to her husband, "Get Elaina's bag from the front-hall closet and put it in the car. Mom, let's get the kids. Lionetta, you and Sophia go package up some food, and we'll take this party to the hospital."

"Thanks, Kate," Elaina said.

"I'll keep them busy," Kate said, and Elaina grasped her hand before her sister-in-law went to corral the children.

Tyler knelt beside her and gently rubbed her tight belly. "I love you."

"Oh, honey, I love you, too."

"We're going to have a baby tonight," he marveled.

"Looks that way."

He smiled and kissed her. Around him a dozen people rushed to get ready, and yet when Elaina gripped his hand hard, Tyler held her.

"This is gonna hurt."

"I wish I could take the pain for you."

"So do I, believe me." She gasped with pain, and Tyler lifted her in his arms, carrying her out to the car.

Six hours later, Elaina Honora Giovanni McKay presented him with a beautiful baby girl, and as Tyler held his daughter, naming her Honora after his wife's great-grandmother, he knew instant, unconditional love. He looked across the bed at Elaina, then placed the baby in her arms. Mother and daughter cuddled, the baby's flame-red hair peeping out from a knit cap. Lane patted the space beside her and Tyler curled up in the bed with his family. The two people he loved most were in his arms, and he felt humbled by the love he felt. These two females had captured his heart at first sight.

A man didn't stand a chance around a redhead.

"Merry Christmas, sweetheart," he said.

"I bet you're the first in this town to get a baby for Christmas," Elaina whispered tiredly, and felt his chuckle rumble against her. "But then, you're always trying to show people up."

"I try." He slipped a thin diamond bracelet from his pocket and fastened it on her wrist.

Elaina gasped at the beauty of it. "Tyler, see? You're such a show-off." And she was glad of it.

He smiled tenderly, his emotions glittering in his eyes. "Thank you, Elaina. You've made me a very happy man."

A tear rolled down her cheek. "Oh, darling, you've given me my dreams."

"Funny how our dreams are the same, huh?" He kissed her hand where his rings sparkled.

"It's amazing what effect the words *go away* had on you," she whispered, touching his jaw as he smiled that irresistible McKay smile. Elaina had had no idea when she'd let him into her life, into her heart, that it was the start of something glorious, that for the rest of their lives they'd celebrate love and happiness.

The past was gone, reborn with a love that grew by the minute, and as she gazed into his blue eyes, she knew, it was the stuff made for legends.

* * * * *

SOCIAL GRACES
by Dixie Browning
(Silhouette Desire #1550)

While struggling to prove his brother's innocence in a corporate scandal, can a rugged marine archaeologist resist his sizzling attraction to the pampered socialite who might be involved in the crime?

*Available December 2003
at your favorite retail outlet.*

Visit Silhouette at www.eHarlequin.com   SDSG

✂

Your opinion is important to us! Please take a few moments to share your
thoughts with us about your experiences with Harlequin and Silhouette books.
Your comments will be very useful in ensuring that we deliver books you love to read.
***Please take a few minutes to complete the questionnaire,
then send it to us at the address below.***

Send your completed questionnaires to:
Harlequin/Silhouette Reader Survey, P.O. Box 9046, Buffalo, NY 14269-9046

1. As you may know, there are many different lines under the Harlequin and Silhouette
brands. Each of the lines is listed below. Please check the box that most represents
your reading habit for each line.

Line	Currently read this line	Do not read this line	Not sure if I read this line
Harlequin American Romance	❏	❏	❏
Harlequin Duets	❏	❏	❏
Harlequin Romance	❏	❏	❏
Harlequin Historicals	❏	❏	❏
Harlequin Superromance	❏	❏	❏
Harlequin Intrigue	❏	❏	❏
Harlequin Presents	❏	❏	❏
Harlequin Temptation	❏	❏	❏
Harlequin Blaze	❏	❏	❏
Silhouette Special Edition	❏	❏	❏
Silhouette Romance	❏	❏	❏
Silhouette Intimate Moments	❏	❏	❏
Silhouette Desire	❏	❏	❏

2. Which of the following best describes why you bought *this book?* One answer only,
please.

the picture on the cover	❏	the title	❏
the author	❏	the line is one I read often	❏
part of a miniseries	❏	saw an ad in another book	❏
saw an ad in a magazine/newsletter	❏	a friend told me about it	❏
I borrowed/was given this book	❏	other: _____	❏

3. Where did you buy *this book?* One answer only, please.

at Barnes & Noble	❏	at a grocery store	❏
at Waldenbooks	❏	at a drugstore	❏
at Borders	❏	on eHarlequin.com Web site	❏
at another bookstore	❏	from another Web site	❏
at Wal-Mart	❏	Harlequin/Silhouette Reader	
at Target	❏	Service/through the mail	❏
at Kmart	❏	used books from anywhere	❏
at another department store or mass merchandiser	❏	I borrowed/was given this book	❏

4. On average, how many Harlequin and Silhouette books do you buy at one time?

I buy _____ books at one time	❏
I rarely buy a book	❏

MRQ403SD-1A

5. How many times per month do you shop for any *Harlequin and/or Silhouette* books?
One answer only, please.

1 or more times a week ❑   a few times per year ❑
1 to 3 times per month ❑   less often than once a year ❑
1 to 2 times every 3 months ❑   never ❑

6. When you think of your ideal heroine, which *one* statement describes her the best?
One answer only, please.

She's a woman who is strong-willed   ❑   She's a desirable woman ❑
She's a woman who is needed by others   She's a powerful woman ❑
She's a woman who is taken care of   ❑   She's a passionate woman ❑
She's an adventurous woman   ❑   She's a sensitive woman ❑

7. The following statements describe types or genres of books that you may be
interested in reading. Pick *up to 2 types* of books that you are most interested in.

I like to read about truly romantic relationships ❑
I like to read stories that are sexy romances ❑
I like to read romantic comedies ❑
I like to read a romantic mystery/suspense ❑
I like to read about romantic adventures ❑
I like to read romance stories that involve family ❑
I like to read about a romance in times or places that I have never seen ❑
Other: _____ ❑

*The following questions help us to group your answers with those readers who are
similar to you. Your answers will remain confidential.*

8. Please record your year of birth below.
19 ____

9. What is your marital status?

single ❑   married ❑   common-law ❑   widowed ❑
divorced/separated ❑

10. Do you have children 18 years of age or younger currently living at home?

yes ❑   no ❑

11. Which of the following best describes your employment status?

employed full-time or part-time ❑   homemaker ❑   student ❑
retired ❑   unemployed ❑

12. Do you have access to the Internet from either home or work?

yes ❑   no ❑

13. Have you ever visited eHarlequin.com?

yes ❑   no ❑

14. What state do you live in?

_____

15. Are you a member of Harlequin/Silhouette Reader Service?

yes ❑   Account # _____   no ❑   MRQ403SD-1B

eHARLEQUIN.com

The eHarlequin.com online community is *the* place to share opinions, thoughts and feelings!

- Joining the community is easy, fun and **FREE!**

- Connect with **other romance fans** on our message boards.

- Meet your **favorite authors** without leaving home!

- **Share opinions** on books, movies, celebrities…and *more!*

Here's what our members say:

"I love the friendly and helpful atmosphere filled with support and humor."
—Texanna (eHarlequin.com member)

"Is this the place for me, or what? There is nothing I love more than 'talking' books, especially with fellow readers who are reading the same ones I am."
—Jo Ann (eHarlequin.com member)

**Join today by visiting
www.eHarlequin.com!**

INTCOMM

If you enjoyed what you just read,
then we've got an offer you can't resist!

Take 2 bestselling
love stories FREE!
Plus get a FREE surprise gift!

Clip this page and mail it to Silhouette Reader Service™

IN U.S.A.
3010 Walden Ave.
P.O. Box 1867
Buffalo, N.Y. 14240-1867

IN CANADA
P.O. Box 609
Fort Erie, Ontario
L2A 5X3

YES! Please send me 2 free Silhouette Desire® novels and my free surprise gift. After receiving them, if I don't wish to receive anymore, I can return the shipping statement marked cancel. If I don't cancel, I will receive 6 brand-new novels every month, before they're available in stores! In the U.S.A., bill me at the bargain price of $3.57 plus 25¢ shipping and handling per book and applicable sales tax, if any*. In Canada, bill me at the bargain price of $4.24 plus 25¢ shipping and handling per book and applicable taxes**. That's the complete price and a savings of at least 10% off the cover prices—what a great deal! I understand that accepting the 2 free books and gift places me under no obligation ever to buy any books. I can always return a shipment and cancel at any time. Even if I never buy another book from Silhouette, the 2 free books and gift are mine to keep forever.

225 SDN DNUP
326 SDN DNUQ

Name	(PLEASE PRINT)	
Address	Apt.#	
City	State/Prov.	Zip/Postal Code

* Terms and prices subject to change without notice. Sales tax applicable in N.Y.
** Canadian residents will be charged applicable provincial taxes and GST.
  All orders subject to approval. Offer limited to one per household and not valid to
  current Silhouette Desire® subscribers.
® are registered trademarks of Harlequin Books S.A., used under license.

DES02   ©1998 Harlequin Enterprises Limited

DYNASTIES: THE BARONES

An extraordinary miniseries featuring the powerful and wealthy Barones of Boston, an elite clan caught in a web of danger, deceit and...desire!

PASSIONATELY EVER AFTER
by Metsy Hingle
(Silhouette Desire #1549)

Discover a love so great— the secret affair between a pregnant Barone beauty and her older, millionaire Conti lover—it can end a long-standing feud and a family curse....

Available December 2003 at your favorite retail outlet.

Visit Silhouette at www.eHarlequin.com   SDDYNNPAE

COMING NEXT MONTH

SDCNM1103

ALLEN COUNTY PUBLIC LIBRARY

3 1833 05568 2444

...o. *Close your eyes,*" he ordered.

Cady bristled. "Who do you think—"

"Just do it."

And she found herself obeying, as much out of surprise as anything. Her heart thudded in her chest. He was right in front of her; she could feel him, sense the heat from his body.

"Open your mouth."

Pulse jittery, she did.

"Tell me what you think of this," he murmured. His fingers were hard and warm against her lips and cheek. Then she stilled, because he slipped a tidbit of something into her mouth that smelled incredible.

And tasted even better.

She bit down, and exquisite flavor burst through her mouth. She wanted more. She couldn't prevent a humming moan of pleasure.

"I take it that means you approve."

Her eyes flew open to see Damon standing there, staring at her, intent.

He watched her with the eyes of a man who'd just pleasured a woman, not with taste but with touch.

AUG 1 4 2008   ROMANCE

Dear Reader,

My name is Kristin and I'm a cookaholic. I used to think I could quit anytime I want, but now I have to admit it—I'm obsessed. Maybe I should blame my mother, who let me watch *Galloping Gourmet* reruns when I was home sick as a kid, or my high-school teacher, who introduced me to Julia Child. At any rate, it was only a matter of time before I wrote a book about a chef, which, of course, required me to finagle my way into a five-star-restaurant kitchen. Purely for research purposes, of course. Several months and several hundred dollars' worth of cooking gear later (Japanese turning mandoline! Timbale molds! Immersion circulator!), this book was born.

I'd love to hear what you think of Cady and Damon and the rest of the McBains, so drop me a line at Kristin@kristinhardy.com. And don't forget to watch for the stories of Max, Walker and Tucker, coming soon. In the meantime, stop by www.kristinhardy.com for news, recipes and contests, or to sign up for my newsletter informing readers of new releases.

Enjoy!

Kristin Hardy